OUTLAWS PUBLISHING

DED

SCOTT HOWEY

CHAPTER 1

"Seventeen." The dealer's voice was loud and harsh. It had to be for the noise of the Western Palace was unbearable for those with a sensitive ear. There were dance hall ladies on the stage lifting their skirts to the cheers and whistles of the drunken cowboys and ill-bred townsfolk. To his right men fell across the bar. Sporting women leaning close, making temporary promises of eternal love. A short, square bald bartender moved lithely tending to the patrons, sweat beading on his thick forehead.

"Twelve." Moans of disappointment mingled with a lone cry of excitement from the roulette table. The house was winning. The house always won. Standing on the second floor and leaning against the balcony, the owners of the establishment cast their inquisitive eyes on the scene. The stranger tried to guess what they were talking about, and even though he could not understand what they were saying he knew it was something about fleecing some poor soul out of their earnings.

A woman, clad in a voluptuous red dress sat opposite

him. Her bosom struggled to be set free. Her fiery red hair was piled on top of her head, yet like her bosom urged to be let loose. Her voice was as slippery as tar, "what's your name sweetheart?"

He stared at her and mused silently. He hadn't had a better offer for some time; besides, she didn't look too bad. Female company would be good for a change. "Tim, Tim Noble."

She slurred her words. "Ain't you a handsome one."

He'd been called handsome before by every whore in every town that wanted his money. It was all part of the game; besides, he knew very well he wasn't handsome. The man had enough respect for himself to accept the facts for what they were. "What's your name, sugar?"

She cooed like a woman half her age. "You can call me Doris."

"Well, Doris, what'll be your pleasure?"

"I could ask you the same question." Her voice was lurid, and she raised her thick eyebrows at him. "Do you have something in mind?" She shuffled her chair closer and rested her hand on his thigh.

It was then that he got a whiff of her. She smelled of

sex and sweat. It was a concoction he didn't favor unless he participated in bringing on the sweat.

The dealer called out again. The dance girls stopped for a break and just when he thought the world would quieten down, a rangy looking rapscallion began tinkling the keys of the piano. That was it, he had enough. It was time to leave. "You're too late, sweetheart."

He stood and she followed his move and stepped after him. Doris grabbed him by the shirt sleeve and tried to turn him around. He shrugged her off, and her drunkenness caused her to trip over a chair and crash to the floor.

He strode across the floor and pushed his way through the batwings. The muffled sound of an unfolding chaos echoed in the room beyond. As he stepped down into the street the cool night air greeted his face. He breathed deeply and stretched. It was time to find a place to rest. He would ride out of town, find a quiet place off the road, and curl up by a cold fire and try to get some shut eye.

He reached for the reins of his roan that had been waiting patiently out front of the Palace when a gnarled and angry voice halted his movements.

"What do you think you're doing?"

A shiver ran down his spine. He turned and saw an ugly looking man on the top stair. Doris was behind him, struggling to maintain her dignity and pointing an accusatory figure at the stranger into town. "That's him. He is the one that threw me to the ground. All because I rejected his advances."

He turned and squared up to the intruder. There was no use trying to convince anyone he was innocent of such a charge. A few patrons, alerted to the possibility of a fracas stepped out of the Palace and spread along the wall. A sulky stopped on the other side of the street heading east. A man and a woman sat patiently, waiting for the action to begin.

CHAPTER 2

The stranger's name is Timothy Noble. He was a local of Littlefield, a small community north-west of Lubbock. He grew up on a spread six miles east of the city. His father was a preacher and his mother a dutiful wife. They lived an ideal life, well that is the life they presented in public. In private they were alcoholics and slept in separate beds. It was a cold and loveless marriage. One born of convenience and duty. His father's name was William McMasters Noble. Shyster is not the right word to describe his personality, neither is carpetbagger, but he was shiftier than the breeze on a warm evening. William dappled in stolen horseflesh and had part shares in a bootlegging operation. He had been forced out of more towns than he could remember. Once he married and settled down and was blessed with a son, he changed a little.

His mother's name was Mary Anne Lee (nee). She was as cold as ice on a winter morning, and he felt every rejection she handed him. It was a loveless house. He was an inconvenience. An only child, he spent time keeping himself entertained. He learned to read early and was adept at Latin, but this had no purpose in a contemporary society. One in which people could make their riches from working hard and believing in Christ.

His father had the gift of the gab. He was a marvelous storyteller. He had a way of reading the room and either inciting his flock to anger or tears, depending on his need for them at the time. He was schooled at home by his mother who was a strict disciplinarian, and he copped his share of whacks across the knuckles from a wooden ruler.

His mother died of tuberculosis when he was twelve. It was a painful death. She coughed and coughed until she bled, and then she would fall into a deep sleep, only to wake and start coughing again. She was removed from the house on a bleak, gray and wet day. His father promised they would see her again soon, but he never saw her again. He didn't even get to stand by her grave at a funeral and weep. Despite the failings of his parents, he loved them. It was a bond born out of misery, and only a connection he could understand, if he had a mind to.

Life with his father was intolerable. The preacher

stopped preaching and spent more time and energy into the bootlegging business. He lost his touch with words, for alcohol will often skew your values and erode the skills you possessed. He was a wreck and slept little. Somehow, he attracted another wife, by the name of Margaret Fontaine. Their marriage was a shambles. They drank together and when they weren't fighting, they were sleeping. Those with the same qualities of character tend to find one another. Such were the new couple. By this time Noble, which he had come to be known by the locals, had grown quite considerably. He tended to his education, by reading the bible mostly. He developed a black and white view of the world. There was right and wrong. There was no need to look any further. The word of God was sacrosanct, and such a view persisted for years, but like all thing's life has a habit of getting in the way of dreams and childhood fancies.

His father and stepmother died on his twentieth birthday. They were found riddled with bullets outside their burning barn. It was the same barn in which he kept his distillery. Rumors abound that the Nobles were murdered by Billy Taggart and his brother Wild Buck.

They were of course in competition for the illegal moonshine business and the struggle had come to the fore. The younger Noble decided to pay no attention to the rumors, and after inheriting the family place he sold it to Avery Thomas for a pretty penny. He saddled his roan, tied what meagre belongings he had to the horse and left Littlefield behind. He vowed never to return.

CHAPTER 3

That was five years ago.

He was a young man. Alone in the world, and unsure of his future. He turned his hand to ranching, but his soft upbringing had turned him off such labor. He was fired before he could muster the strength and courage to quit. A year after leaving home he found himself camping on a river in a makeshift town called Telegraph. There was no telegraph at Telegraph, it was merely rumored to be the place where they cut down poles to make the telegraph lines for the rest of the country. It was small enough to be insignificant in the grand scheme of the American west, but to the people that called it home it meant something, just what that was no one could ever tell. The people of Telegraph came from all walks of life. It wasn't washed with high class establishments. There was merely a store, a post office and a drinking and pleasure establishment. The last two, like most of the dwellings that passed for homes were hastily constructed out of canvas, and timber that was plentiful in the area.

He spent most of his time fishing and hunting. He made some acquaintances which soon worked out his vulnerabilities and exploited him for what he was worth. Naive and a little slow to anger he found himself the butt of many jokes. He loved the company of men and women, regardless of their status in society. It was simply because he was starved of love when he was a child. Despite his parents' religious mindset, he soon abandoned his values. He turned to ladies of comfort and to whiskey. Why not? It was what everyone else was doing.

In Lubbock, Post, Sweetwater, Brady and Eden men and women indulged in vice. Gambling, drinking, whoring, and crime. From petty theft and robbery to murder. People of all walks of life were pursuing their pleasure. For some it was land and power. For others it was money, well for most it was money. He absorbed the world around him like a dry sponge soaking up the rain. He moved slowly, was eager to please and had many acquaintances. But such a life leads to no long-lasting relationships. At best, the people that came into his life were temporary, and gone again. Some died, like Jasper Taff. He was a gentle old man he met on the riverbank outside of Telegraph. He got drunk one night and fell into the river that streaked its way through the earth. They found his body a quarter of a mile downstream. His lungs were full of water and his pockets were empty.

Noble was an amicable lad, and easy going. But he was turning hard. He was tired of always having to listen, and not be listened to. He found himself giving both money and advice and only one was ever accepted. Money was no issue for the man, yet it never is for those that have it. He made a pot when he sold the family home and because his wants were meager, he would never have to worry about fare for some time to come. What grilled Noble's chops was the death of a prostitute?

Delores, the whore he had vowed to love forever. The same woman he planned to leave Telegraph with and start a future together, was found in her tent, on a thin mattress, under the covers of a dirty sheet with several knife wounds to the chest and her throat slashed. That was a week ago, and the reason he left Telegraph behind. They would spend time laughing and planning a future, and Delores thought it romantic, but many whores and their tricks live in a fantasy world. It comes with the price. It wasn't until she worked out that the boy that doted over her was no regular John, but also a wealthy one that she committed to making plans. Quite often dreams remain unfulfilled and so it was, that as Delores was lowered into a pauper's grave by the banks of the river, Noble after five years hiatus turned to the good book. He read the Lord's Prayer and stood in silence for twice as long as he did for his father. Without a care in the world, and without looking back, he rode out of the place he called home.

He left Telegraph with a pocket full of memories and a head full of bitterness.

CHAPTER 4

"What have you got to say for yourself, Boy?"

Noble was wide across the shoulder and ran straight down to the hip. Standing at three inches over six feet, he cut an imposing figure. Yet one look at his face tempted men to goad him. He was almost bald at twenty-five, and his face sported wisps of hair, but one couldn't say that he had a beard nor could one with confidence argue that he didn't. His eyes were big and his lips fleshy. Despite his size he looked boyish. The contrast made him an easy target, and he had suffered a beating or two over the years. The beatings were quite simply because he didn't fight back. Of all the vices he witnessed over the years violence was one he couldn't abide. Sure, gambling was risky, yet filled him with an energy he wanted to grasp hold onto and not let go. After several heavy losses though he steered away from such pastime activities.

Whoring was fun. Pleasurable to say the least. Drinking was also, in moderation, an enjoyable pastime, but violence? Well, he saw no pleasure in violence. It was in Brady a few years ago he copped his first whooping. Joseph Tombs broke his nose, and to this day he didn't even know why. Probably because he felt like it. That was the type of man Tombs was. He'd pick someone weaker than himself and let loose. A bully. A thug. What made it worse is that Tombs was the sheriff of Brady at the time.

Then there was a time in Telegraph he got a little too liquored up and woke up with some bruises. He didn't worry too much about this licking because he reasoned that he deserved it for imbibing in too much moonshine. Still, the thought of violence didn't sit well with him. Now he could sense that he would have to stand down again. He always did. He did so in Lubbock, and in Snyder. In every town he went to he found himself embroiled in some drama. Some of it was his doing, yet most of it not so.

"Are you deaf, boy?" The man who stepped down into the street emphasized the last word to incite the lad into action.

Noble straightened. "Excuse me, Sir?"

The man stepped closer. He stood three inches over Noble. His face was matted with an unruly beard, and he smelled of beer, whiskey, and smoke. He snarled and when he did Noble could see meat between his teeth. "Sir? Are you some kind of gentleman, BOY?"

The insults weren't lost on the other man, but he let them slide. He had always let them slide. "Pardon me?"

The man was close now, too close. Noble felt that same familiar feeling of fear sweep through him. Trouble was at hand and there was nothing he could do but accept another licking.

"Apologize to the lady?"

Doris was standing on the top step, in her red dress. Her hands held delicately in front of her. Her knight in shining armor was set to wreak revenge on the man who had wronged her, and she was looking forward to it.

Noble was genuinely baffled. "What lady?"

The crowd, which had swelled quite considerably, chuckled. Doris blushed with anger, as did her rescuer. The antagonizer stepped close and through clenched teeth muttered. "You knocked the lady over, now apologize."

He did what he had always done. He apologized to his mother for the slightest infringement, real or imagined. He apologized to his father to avoid the belt.

He apologized in Lubbock. He apologized in Brady, and he apologized in Telegraph, and so out of habit he apologized to the lady in Rocksprings.

"I'm sorry for knocking you over."

CHAPTER 5

The crowd laughed. Their derision echoed in the night air. All around him, a mirth of laughter caught his ears. From behind, the man on the sulky guffawed and chuffed. A short rotund man to the right of Doris choked on his cigar smoke. A smirk spread across his face like water across the barren earth. When the smoke cleared, he could hear the man's antagonizing laughter. Doris smiled and looked from side to side. She bared her teeth, threw her head back and cackled like a witch. The man in front of him. The ugly man laughed the loudest, baring his teeth in a meaty smirk and then suddenly, the laughter stopped as Noble fell to his knees courtesy of a headbutt from the antagonizer. Blood trickled from a cut above his right eye.

His head was spinning. He felt sick in the stomach.

"Dag-nabit, Jake. The man apologized. Why did you have to do that?" A lone voice from somewhere in the distance caught Noble's ear. Other voices not so pliable to his cause found his dazed and confused mind.

"Make an example of him?" Doris encouraged her

champion.

"Beat him to a pulp." Screamed another.

"Kick him. Punch him." Screamed a child, no more than ten.

Noble managed the cobwebs, reached out for the hitchrail, and used it to help him stand. Buoyed by the eagerness of the crowd, Jake decided to bask in his moment of glory. With one slow yet forceful kick the injured man's legs fell from beneath him, and he thudded into the dust. More laughter. Cackling. More threats. All he wanted to do was get on his mount and leave. There was no need for violence. He despised violence. He let go of an involuntary oath when his attacker grabbed him by the little hair he had and dragged him through the dirt to the water trough. He tried to break free, but all his strength had escaped him.

He felt the anguish at his dilemma. All he wanted was some female company, yet when push came to shove, he couldn't tend to his affairs. It wasn't the woman named Doris as much as it was the woman he left behind in a cold grave in Telegraph.

Visions of Delores played across his mind. She was

the only person who listened to him. She doted on him. Took him seriously as a man. His mother never did. She derided and insulted him. His father threatened him, and he cowered away in fright. He always cowered away in fright. In Lubbock. In Brady and in every two-bit place where men needed to prove themselves. He stepped aside. He always gave way. He had been called a coward on more than one occasion. His manhood questioned. His courage was tested and at each moment in which men felt the need to push, torment and harass him, he walked away. The faces of those that had belittled and tormented him flashed through his mind, but they were soon washed away as his body was jerked upward and his face submerged into the water.

He struggled to break free, but the man was too strong. He tried to hold his breath, but he swallowed water instead. Just when he thought he was going to drown he was released and he managed to suck air, but his reprieve was short lived. He was soon struggling beneath the water again. Then suddenly, he broke free in the most startling of circumstances. He was overcome with a feeling so intense that he didn't even know where it came from. It consumed his body like a fire. From head to toe. His heart was aching. His mind was racing yet focused. He placed his hands on the edge of the trough to brace himself and forced his head out of the water. Despite his attackers' will to do so he could not force Noble's head under the water. He let out an almighty scream that startled his attacker and the onlookers.

CHAPTER 6

He screamed so loud that it startled even himself. With all the strength he could muster he pushed himself off the trough and stood. At the same time, he shook his head like a rabid dog tearing at a carcass. Jake released his grip and stepped back. Noble cursed and turned as Jake stepped back. He screamed as loud as he could. The noise split the air in a volcanic rush. The onlookers covered their ears. He held his arms by his side. His chest puffed out. Eyes wide. His mouth agape. His pupils enlarged. Fists clenched.

For the first time that evening Jake felt fear pass from his head to his feet. He could not run. His feet went numb. Even if he could move, pride and reputation would root him to the spot. His look was a fusion of mystery, fear, and confusion. It wasn't supposed to be this way. Without saying a word Noble stepped forward and threw a right cross that hit Jake on the chin. The man fell like a sack of potatoes. It was a vicious strike. Born of twenty-five years of neglect. Of running. Of hiding in the shadows. Of abuse.

Jake hit the ground hard. His body curled to the ground like a dropped towel. The crowd doubled in size. Most of Rocksprings arrived just in time for the greatest spectacle the town had seen. They let out an audible gasp. It was a concoction of surprise and horror. Despite being stunned by the blow Jake managed to scramble to his feet. Noble stepped forward while the other raised his fists. He was too late. A left jab followed by a straight right to the forehead dropped him again.

The blood and water on Noble's face ran as one. His face appeared covered in blood. His crooked teeth snarled as he threw himself on the prone figure. He sat upon his chest, pining Jake's arms. Drool dribbled out of his mouth as he became consumed with anger. He reached out his left hand and grabbed him by the hair, lifted his head and punched him in the nose.

An arc of blood followed a guttural groan. A red mist hung in the air. The crowd gasped. Doris screamed. Another woman closer to the action fainted. Jake lay unconscious as Noble unleashed with another solid right to the mouth. Teeth splintered and cracked. He let go of the man's hair and straddled atop him proceeded to unleash with a series of blows. Each blow a sickening thud. Blood flowed off his hands as he raised them in preparation for another punch to the unconscious man. He had lost control. Years of crawling. Of running away. Of cowardice. The built-up hate and frustration flowed out of his fists and into Jake's face.

A bystander, witnessing the carnage called out in both anger and confusion. "Stop. The men had enough."

Noble didn't hear, but even if he did, he showed no indication of heeding the man's words. He was punching a piece of meat now. Jake's face was a wet, mushy piece of meat. The sound of the blows echoed in the night. The stranger called again. Men and women looked away. While others peered for a closer look. Doris stepped into the street and screamed at the attacker, but it was no use. He was oblivious to everyone else. Consumed by the moment. Filled with rage.

The man yelled again. "That's enough. Stop." This time his expression was more direct. He stepped off the landing, scurried across to the unfolding scene and tried to pull Noble off his victim. He failed. Despite his size he couldn't budge the attacker. Noble was like a hungry wolf set upon its prey.

Then suddenly Noble's world turned black.

CHAPTER 7

The sun rose in Rocksprings upon a cautious day. In a small yard on the outskirts of town half a dozen cows mooed lazily. A rooster, perched on a weathered cross brace crowed restlessly. A lone rider heading for Telegraph, looking a little worse for wear, rubbed his eyes and yawned. News traveled fast. It wouldn't be long before the events of the night before would be told and retold in contrasting manners. The truth is the victim of a good story. Those in Telegraph would be stunned to hear what unfolded in the peaceful town of Rocksprings a hundred miles south.

An elderly woman stepped onto the porch of her run-down abode. The crooked planks squeaked as she carried a bucket full of dirty water to the edge of the porch and threw it into the street. She looked east and west, spat, and cursed the day. The door slammed behind her. A crow set sail from the church's bell and glided through the street. A mangy cur searched the alley for scraps, sniffed the earth in a vain request to satisfy its endless hunger. A tall, rangy man moved languidly along the porch out front of the corner store. In his hands was a straw broom. He swept aimlessly. The dust rising and falling in the same spot. He was weary and stooped with age. It was a tedious chore, performed out of routine rather than with any distinct purpose.

A middle-aged man, dressed in a dappled pinstripe suit, and donning a derby hat walked past. He was Joe Denning, the local banker and one of two local lawyers. Amicable enough if he was left to chew on the world in private.

"Morning, Joe."

"Morning, Ned."

They stood facing each other, like they had for every morning for the last twelve years. "Hear about the fight last night?"

"Sure enough. Hard to fathom why a man would do such a thing."

Ned leaned on the broom. "What's happening with the world, Joe?"

The man just shook his head and shrugged his shoulders. "Doesn't pay to ponder on such things, Ned."

Ned shook his head and went back to sweeping.

"Yes, sir, I suppose you're right Joe. I suppose you're right."

Denning continued his journey. Head down and feeling sick and tired of Rocksprings. The place was becoming claustrophobic. A door banged. The sound startled him, and he looked to his left. Percy Billings stepped into the day, stretched, and relieved himself. Denning shook his head. Yes sir, it was time to leave.

A horse whinnied; its owner thoughtlessly left the mount in front of the Palace all night. He stopped and tried to rerun the images of the fight the night before through his mind. There was no evidence. No scuff marks and no blood. The scene had been tendered to. The honorable and righteous folks of Rocksprings, of which there seemed to be less and less, were protected from such atrocities. A window above him opened, and a woman leaned the top half of her body through. Her hair disheveled. Her bosom pale, yet despite the hour inviting. She saw the banker and taking every opportunity to make a dollar, propositioned him. When he turned away from her, she laughed and disappeared. The breeze picked up and played with the faded white curtains.

The sign to the sheriff's office moved gently. The steps squeaked as the man's large frame tramped up them to the door. He fumbled with a key. His hands were cold. He opened the door and stepped inside. The door slammed behind him.

Meanwhile, like ants, the folks of Rocksprings had come alive. They scoured across the street. There were chores to be done. Errands to be run. People to see. Conversations to be had. Though life in Rocksprings moved slowly, gossip moved quickly.

CHAPTER 8

Sheriff Otis Wells spent the night at the office. However, he just returned from home, a block away where his dutiful wife made him breakfast. 7:00 am every morning breakfast was served. Bacon, eggs, and toast. He was a predictable lawman, who not only liked his creature comforts, but thrived on routine. He tended to the fire in the corner of the large room. He was addicted to coffee and drank it like water. After the essential preparations, the kindling sparked, and he moved across to his desk and sat down.

He was a large man, carrying too much weight around the middle. He sported a thick, and uneven mustache that drooped awkwardly over fleshy lips. His brow was stern and that fitted his demeanor. He shuffled some papers, retrieved a pencil, and licked its tip before writing feverishly. The office was large and consisted of the desk opposite the fireplace and a large cell in the north-eastern corner of the room. There wasn't much need for the law in Rocksprings. It was a peaceful town. The odd drunk here and there, some petty theft, but nothing like what happened less than twelve hours ago.

The scratching of the pencil on paper was relaxing. A deep silence pervaded the room. The fire passed the point of no return, and Wells paused briefly to stoke the furnace. He readied the coffee pot, and set it atop the furnace, cast a wary glance at the prisoner and moved to the window. To his left, the bald barman, Mince, stood in front of the batwings of the Western Palace smoking a cigarette. His apron was stained. He looked nervous, but it was the nature of the man. He heard laughter emanating from the window on the second floor of the Palace. 'Blasted whores,' he thought to himself. They bring just as much heartache as they do pleasure.

To his right Ned was leaning on his broom talking to Mavis Williams. Mavis was the town's biggest gossip. She was never out this early, and when she turned and looked at the law office while Ned pointed, Wells quickly surmised the reason for gracing the morning at this hour.

Wells moved across to the gun cabinet on the wall above his desk. He fumbled with the key for the chain that ran through the gun guards, unlocked them, and removed the Greener. Locking the guns in place he moved to his desk and opened the bottom draw. He loaded the shotgun and placed some spares in his pockets. Laying the gun on the desk he moved across to the coffee pot, laid the back of his hand across the enamel and, deciding it was hot enough, removed his cup from the hook on the wall near the fire.

Otis Wells was no fool. He knew the score. The events were too sensational to keep secret. He also knew that Jake had some pardners, who just may consider the need to seek some form of revenge. The saving grace is that they lived twelve miles away at a place called Miller's Mines. They were named after Maxuel Miller, the man who discovered them, played them out and sold the rights to Jake and his outfit several years earlier. Truth is that Miller made next to nothing. He sold the outfit a dream and they were eager to part with money with the hope of striking it rich. Jake's partners would know by now what has transpired on a dark night in the main street of Rocksprings. They would make a grand entrance and they would seek a reckoning. It is not every day that a pardner gets murdered.

CHAPTER 9

Noble was awake when the sheriff entered. His head hurt, and he tried to recollect what had happened. He remembered most of what transpired. He recalled Doris, and her scent of sweat. He also remembered leaving, and of course being accosted by the stranger. He breathed deeply and when he exhaled, he recalled his head being dunked under water. The laughter. He started to burn inside. Anger welled within him. It surprised him, so he closed his eyes tighter and tried to force it away. It was hard. He opened his eyes and moaned. The light pierced his eyes and his head throbbed. Sitting up in his bed, he blinked three times and held his hands before his eyes. They were covered in dry blood. Lots of blood. It was down his forearms and underneath his fingernails. He appeared shocked and looked through the steel bars at the back of the man who was looking out the wide window that stretched across the front of the room. "Where am I?" His voice was hesitant, and he repeated himself as he stood and made his way to the cell bars. "Where am I?"

"You're in jail, Boy."

He stuttered. "J... jail? For what?"

The lawman sat on the edge of his desk. "Murder."

Noble sat on the edge of the bed. Head in his hands. Thoughts racing. The noise. The laughter. Images of the man flashed through his mind. The water. He peered at the lawman. "What happened?"

"Well Son," the sheriff said moving from his desk across to the cell door, " you beat a man to death with your fists."

Noble remembered the confrontation, but that's all he remembered. "You mean, he's dead?"

"That's right. You killed him."

He rubbed his head. "I don't remember. I just don't remember." Wells watched the man closely. He had heard excuses before, but not like this. Not for murder. Men get drunk and do stuff they don't remember. Women as well, but it's the first time he heard about it to this extent. He figured the man's memory would come back at a convenient time. The door opened and a short, thin man entered. He wore corduroy pants, a long sleeve plaid shirt and red braces. He sported spectacles which perched precariously on the end of his nose.

"Good morning, Sheriff."

"Morning, Walter. I have those telegrams and letters ready."

The small man reached out to take the letters. "Not a word to a soul, Walter."

"I know the drill, Sheriff. I won't say a word and I will burn the telegrams when I am done."

"Thanks, Walter."

Walter cast a cautious eye at the prisoner and turned his attention back to the sheriff. "He doesn't look like a killer. "

"Well, he is. Hurry on now. Let me know as soon as word comes back."

He nodded and moved through the door but not before looking over his shoulder at the prisoner one last time. Noble was kneeling by the bed. His hands in the praying position. Eyes closed. Head down. Wells watched him intently as he poured himself another coffee. He looked through the window and saw the tall and distinguished figure of Miles Hammond, the newspaperman, make a bee line for his office. He stepped outside and waited for Hammond to make his presence known.

"Howdy, Sheriff."

He had no time for reporters, and less time for Hammond. "Miles."

"Can I get a quote about the events surrounding the death of Jake Jenkins?"

"Sure. Mr. Jenkins was killed in an altercation. The details surrounding the killer's identity and the facts of the case are still to be determined."

"Is that all?"

"That's all I got. I won't know any more until I speak to the witnesses and the accused."

"Thanks, Sheriff, I'll be in touch."

CHAPTER 10

A crowd began gathering out front of the jail. A buzz went around town. There was a rumor that Jake's pardners were coming into town for a lynching. Wells was aware of the sentiment building up outside. He double checked the Greener and made sure it was loaded and stepped onto the porch. He eyed the crowd. His presence drew them out of the woodwork. Despite the day's hour men staggered from the Western Palace and an outrageous curse split the air.

"Hang the buzzard."

Wells nodded contentedly. He was aware of Jake's position in town, and it wasn't swapping stories with the social elite. He was a washed-up cowboy, turned miner. What money he made he spent on liquor and whores. He wasn't a model citizen. In fact, he had been locked up several times for being drunk and disorderly. They were minor offenses, but to hear that he had bullied a stranger in town did not surprise Wells at all.

He stared at them all. A murder of this magnitude in any town would have a ripple effect. In a small town like

Rocksprings the locals are sacrosanct. Love or hate them locals benefitted from the fact that they were local, and when it came to outsiders, well they were never accepted. Finlay Shaw and his family moved to town twenty years ago and were still shunned by the locals. It was an unwritten rule, but one that played out across the American continent. Jake may have been a thug, a bully, a drunk and at times lazy and inconsiderate, but he belonged to Rocksprings. In doing so those that gathered felt a duty to speak up in the man's defense.

"Go home, folks."

The prior phrase was repeated, but this time with more gusto. "Hang the buzzard."

The speaker was Thomas Bland. He was the local butcher, a dolt, and a hot head.

He scanned the crowd for potential troublemakers and concluded that they were there to make a stand only. There would be no violence from them. If it had been an unprovoked attack on a citizen of some note, that would be another matter entirely.

"What do you plan to do, Sheriff?"

"I sent for Wilson Poole. He will watch the prisoner

while I investigate the matter. I have already spoken to some witnesses. Once I gather the evidence, I will decide whether to charge the accused or not."

There was a general uproar. They knew Wells was a strident and determined lawman who always played by the books. He spoke the language and used it well. Still the fact that the accused hadn't been charged yet sent them a stir.

Bland was the loudest, and as is often the case those that are, are most always in the wrong. "I say we hang him now. I was there. I saw it happen. I know who did it."

"You'll do no such thing. Man or woman, I don't care which. Anyone who graces these stairs with their presence to rope the prisoner will get a barrel or two of this." He held the Greener up for the crowd to see, but he wasn't finished talking. As he spoke, he swung the double barrels to the butcher. "Then again, perhaps I'll go to the top of the tree and take out the alpha troublemaker."

Bland swallowed hard. He heard the message.

Wells persisted. "If I hear any more talk of lynching,

I'll arrest you and throw you in the cell with Jake's killer. Now vamoose."

The crowd dispersed. It took five minutes, but they heeded the message. Poole arrived as Wells opened the door.

"Sheriff."

Poole was the sheriff's cousin. He was a capable fellow and followed orders. That's what he needed right now. A solid and dependable deputy. He filled him in on the events that had transpired since the night before. "The star is in the draw, and you are still sworn in from last time. Get your Henry rifle and watch the door. Lock it and make sure no one comes in that you don't trust."

CHAPTER 11

"Where's Doris?"

"Sleeping."

"Wake her up."

"Yes, Sheriff. The bald barman wiped his hands on the towel and discarded it on the bar while he hastened up the stairs.

Wells looked around at the horrendous decor. He was a non-drinker and was content with this arrangement. A drop of alcohol had never passed his lips. He was a strict religious man, and he and his wife Beryl were determined to live a holy life. He had been the sheriff of Rocksprings for four years. He landed in the job after the previous lawman, Jonas Sloan, died of old age. He went to sleep one night and didn't wake up. Wells was approached by representatives of the church and the Chamber of Commerce. He accepted the task of maintaining law and order. Though he didn't always agree that the law could or did deliver justice, he respected the necessity of a legal system. He combined his love of the lord and his respect for the law, and this allowed him to hold down the office in an election two years later.

The barman returned and busied himself with wiping down the bar, and moving onto the tables, and windowsills. "Shouldn't be long now, Sheriff."

"Thanks, Mince."

He heard footsteps approach the top of the stairs. Doris moved quickly down the stairs, and he could hear her ragged breath. "Hello, Sheriff. I'm so glad to see you. I expected as much."

"Doris." He stood and indicated for her to sit.

She mumbled a thanks, fixed her hair and sat down. The lawman removed a pencil and paper from his pocket and began his investigation.

"Can you tell me what happened last night?"

She hesitated, trying to figure what to say, she didn't want to be implicated in the ordeal. "Well, Sheriff, I was walking the floor, you know um, well you know, Sheriff."

"Looking for tricks."

She nodded.

"So, what happened?"

The words fell from her mouth in a rush. "Well, I saw that man, you know the one you knocked out with the barrel of your gun. Well, I asked him if he wanted some company, and he got all hyped up and pushed me over."

"How did Jake get involved?"

"He saw what happened and helped me off the floor. Then he followed the man outside. Once I scrambled off the floor, I followed him."

"What did you do?"

She shrugged her shoulders and looked baffled. "Nothing."

"Did you say anything?"

She tucked hair behind her ears and shook her head. "Nothing."

"To the best of your recollection, recount the series of events that led to Jake's death."

Doris regaled the sheriff with her loose account of the events leading up to her champion's death. It took her ten minutes, and she went through a range of emotions. Meanwhile Wells was scribbling on the pad. When she finished, he continued to write for a minute before looking at her. He didn't believe much of what she said.

He considered lying a sin, and though he felt the urge to lecture her about the evils of her deceit he held his tongue. Instead, he pushed the pad across to her and explained.

"This is your statement, Doris. Please read through it and sign your name."

She looked nervous. "What for?"

He didn't miss a beat, and suddenly, his voice changed tone. "This is an official statement, Doris. By agreeing to and signing this you are declaring that everything in here is true. That's everything."

He handed her the pen, which she moved between her fingers and stared at the statement.

Wells waited a minute before interrupting her train of thought. "Um, is everything alright?"

She couldn't tell him that she had lied in the statement, so she revealed a secret she had been hiding. She leaned forward and whispered. "I can't read or write."

He nodded. Illiteracy was common. "I'll read it to you and if you agree you can make your mark and then we'll get on with the rest of the day."

She nodded. It took him three minutes. She agreed in good faith and made an X.

CHAPTER 12

Wilson Poole sat at the desk. A Henry rifle across his lap. He hadn't spoken a word to the prisoner. He had a dull character, without a sense of humor. He was dreaming when the door rattled. He looked up and saw the large and unforgiving figure of Cletus Cloverfield trying to get into the office. Poole moved swiftly and strode to the door.

"Cletus."

"Howdy, Deputy. I'm here to see the prisoner."

"What for?"

The big man waddled into the room. "I'm here to solicit a client, Deputy."

"Well, sit over there." He pointed to the bench along the wall.

Sheriff Wells climbed the steps and made a loud entrance. He cast his eyes to the intruder. "CC. Looking for business?"

"You know me too well, Sheriff."

Wells laughed at the joke. "You got my letter?"

"You can count on Walter, Sheriff."

He nodded. "I suppose you'll be defending him." He pointed nonchalantly to Noble.

CC's voice was loud. "If he'll have me."

"You're the only lawyer in town that's stepped inside a courtroom. He doesn't have much of a choice."

"Unless he has money. He can buy a fancy lawyer."

"I doubt that a high falutin lawyer would trouble themselves with this case."

"What do you mean?"

He ignored the question. "You're just in time CC. Come with me." The large man followed Wells as he moved to the table and laid the pad and pencil gently on the furnished oak. They stopped in front of the cell door.

"Come here, boy."

Noble moved slowly but did as he was directed.

"What's your name?"

"Noble. Tim Noble."

"Tim Noble, you're under arrest for the murder of Jake Jenkins." Wells continued the rehearsed speech while Cloverfield listened. When he finished Noble laid his head against the bars and cried. The men signed some documents and then CC approached the prisoner. He held out his hand, but he was ignored. My name's Cletus Cloverfield, I am a lawyer, the only decent lawyer in town. I offer my services as your defense attorney. You may decline of course, but the chances of finding someone else to try this case will be difficult. The prosecutor will come into town on the stage a week before the trial. They'll send Maxwell Purcell. He's young, smart, and ambitious, but sharp as a tack. He'll be a tough opponent. I haven't beat him yet, but there's always a first time. If you've got money, you can buy a lawyer from the city, but such people are frowned upon here. No high falutin lawyer has ever won a case in Rocksprings. Now take me for example, I've won as much as I have lost, that's why I'm cheap. That doesn't mean I'm no good. I'm as good as the next lawyer."

"Then why have you lost so much?" Noble was staring at the lawyer, and his gaze caused Cloverfield to pause, catch his breath and manage his thoughts.

"Bias my friend. Simple bias. You see, I am not a local. It is that simple."

"Then why should I hire you?"

"That's easy, because I'm more of a local than anyone else you'll get in this backwater."

He paused and began moving back and forth while his soon to be client watched him intently. He stopped before the prisoner and smiled, "because I can get you off."

Noble was interested. How could he not be? "How?"

CC looked at the sheriff, moved closer to the cell, and whispered. "I'll tell you once you commit to one Cletus Cloverfield as your legal counsel."

In the moment that passed between them Noble summed up the situation. He thought the lawyer was of earth and wind. He was both grounded in the harsh reality of how the legal system works, especially in Rocksprings, yet was an idealist. For a moment he considered hiring an outside lawyer, but he reasoned that Cloverfield was right. The locals didn't like outsiders messing in their affairs. His time in Telegraph taught him many things, one of them being that small towns can be insular and the threat of something and or someone from beyond the city limits could spark a fierce resistance. Less than twenty-four hours ago he rode into town seeking company for a lonely heart and a weary mind. Now he was in jail facing the prospect of jail time or swinging by a rope. He had nothing to lose, except his life and in his state of mind now he didn't much care for it.

He was tossing the idea around in his head when Cloverfield's voice broke the silence.

"I can see you need time to ponder the dilemma, therefore I'll come back in the morning. Meanwhile the lawyers from the city are aware of this situation. They'll be waiting for more information. Once they are informed a prosecutor will be assigned to the case. They'll be the thoroughbred in the race with an early start. If this happens, we won't catch them. You'll be tried and hanged. The law is swift, justice is questionable, and death is certain. The folk of Rocksprings will rise with the day and life will continue. Your name will fade with time, and you'll become nothing but a distant memory. A story to scare the children to behave, to make sure they return home before dark."

Once the lawyer got on a roll, he was hard to stop.

"You're a young man. An innocent man. You're the tributary before it gets to the river. You've got plenty of growing. Life doesn't mean anything if you don't take the chance to try. Life without effort is death. The more you consider the hangman's noose the lonelier you will feel. You'll want to scream. You'll want to cry. You'll want to feel the warmth of a woman. The taste of an expensive whiskey. The cool breeze on your face feels better as a free man. It is crisp. Life giving. Live young man. Embrace the opportunity. Don't cower to the law. You have sinned, as I have, as has the sheriff."

Wells had heard it all before. He looked at CC. The man was good with words, and with the reporter Hammond siding his cause he would make a hell of a noise. Innocent or guilty? In the end it didn't matter. There was something more important at stake here, reputations.

"Your life may not be worth much to you and to the folk out there." He pointed outside. His voice rose and fell with the emotion that guided it. "But it is to me. Your fate is not cast. You are not destined to rot in jail, nor shall you swing from a rope. I know people, sir. Their hopes. Their dreams. Their fears. They stood by the rivers of Jordan to watch while John baptized the Lord Jesus Christ. A new beginning. A cleansing of the soul. A tempering of the spirit. At one with peace. But you're not ready for such a conversion. You are a troubled soul. Lost. Lonely. At times, a fool. Brash and impulsive. Without care, yet receptive to others. You are not a cold-blooded MURDERER."

He almost shouted the last word. It shocked the prisoner, and it was then he saw tears breach the invisible barriers that held them back. Noble wept as the lawyer persisted, though his voice had taken a solemn tone. Moving closer he continued.

"My child. Be not unkind to him that reacheth out his hand. Do not shun me out of fear. For he offereth the world and accepts nothing in return. Listen to your heart. What is it saying? Tell me young man. Listen. Tell me."

A moment of silence passed. CC to his left and Noble behind bars to his right. They were paused in time. Still. Tense. Eerily quiet until the prisoner whispered, "yes."

Wells was grateful. The charade could stop. Yet somehow, he was aware that in fact, it had only just begun.

CHAPTER 13

Darkness fell over Rocksprings and the mood was somber and heavy. The Western Palace was quiet, and the few patrons were content to muse on the vagaries of life in relative silence. Doris was sitting in a chair at a desk propped level by cardboard with a cowboy by the name of Buddy Franks. Franks was a contemporary of Jake Jenkins, but hardly an associate, let alone a friend. One could be forgiven for getting Franks and Deadeye Dave, one of Jake's partners, mixed up. They were uncannily similar. Except for a mole on Frank's face left of his nose, they could be mistaken for identical twins. More light than was needed lit up the room. A handful of patrons either sat laconically around the room or spoke softly.

"I cannot help thinking that it's my fault Jake's dead." Doris uttered the words in a fevered rush. She had not been feeling herself since the interview with the sheriff. She was even more concerned that the lawman had spent the afternoon interviewing other witnesses. Doris was relieved when she found out the stranger in town was arrested and charged with Jake's murder.

Frank's voice was drawn out and weary. "You can't blame yourself, Doris. Jake was doing what he thought was right."

She nodded. She wasn't in the mood for conversation, but she eyed the wrangler up. "Want to go upstairs?"

"I darn well told you Doris, your price has gotten so steep I can't climb that hill anymore."
She smiled, suddenly animated, stood and grabbed him by the hand. "This one is on me."

Franks scrambled to finish his drink and grab his hat before she dragged him away from the table.

At the law office, Cloverfield, the newly appointed defense attorney to Tim Noble sat with his client in the large cell under the furtive gaze of Wilson Poole. The lawyer asked questions about Noble's past. He wanted to know everything about his childhood, and his parents. He wrote feverishly. A picture of the accused was forming in his mind. A defense strategy was developing.

Poole removed his watch from his vest pocket. The dull gold-plated timepiece looked small in the palm of his big hands. He pushed the unlock and the time was revealed. "You have forty minutes left." He would warm them again with ten minutes and two minutes to go. They were the instructions he was given by Wells, and well he always followed instructions.

The sheriff was sitting in his chair by the fire reading the Book of Psalms. He laid the book in his lap and considered Psalm 118:1, *Give thanks unto the Lord; for he is good: because his mercy endureth forever.* He turned the wick down on the lamp, removed his glasses, rubbed his eyes, and closed them.

Miles Hammond was busy ordering around his pressman, Wiley Johns. The Rocksprings Rag was due in the morning, and he had written a piece about the murder and the murderer. He was anticipating a spike in sales, at least while the trial was in progress. The death of Jenkins would make him money and that's all he cared about.

Wiley was as old as time itself, yet he moved lithely. He knew exactly what he was doing and didn't need to be babysat by Hammond. Such motherly attention bothered him, yet he was paid well for his duty. He was old now and his wants and needs were few. Johns lived a solitary life in a well-manicured home with a white picket fence, three blocks from the city center. He was well-respected by his neighbors and a regular at charity events and functions.

Hammond was anxious. The news in town was often hard to generate. He considered the locals a bunch of yokels. He was also an outsider, with a general distaste for life to which he wasn't accustomed. He was from Austin, and with a general interest in writing and with the backing of father's money he bought the Rag, upon the sudden death of the previous owner. That was four years earlier. His intention was to make money, develop a reputation for both his writing and business prowess and move east. It was many a dream for those seeking fame and fortune and Hammond was no different. The only problem was that he left it a little late, and the ravages of age were catching up to him. This is the moment that could make or break his career and his business. He was a thinker. Too much. He would break down a phrase and interpret every syllable. He would count the meter. He would analyze every word to try and understand the true intentions behind people's words and how this reflected their actions. He was an insomniac. His mind raced so fast and in every inconceivable direction that it was difficult to have a meaningful conversation with him. The only person capable of grounding him was the lawyer, Cletus Cloverfield.

Hammond moved back and forth. "Set to print?"

Johns responded, as if he had heard the same questions a thousand times. He anticipated everything. "Almost."

"How long?"

"Five minutes."

Hammond sucked the life out of his cigar, threw the stub on the floor, and killed it with his boot. He patted himself down searching for another and finding none he left Johns and headed back to his office to find another.

Meanwhile, in Austin Texas two-hundred miles east, Maxwell Purcell sat at his oak desk in a plush office on the second floor of the Austin courthouse. He sipped brandy from a snifter glass and picked the piece of paper off his desk and read it for the third. It was a brief prepared by his solicitor assistant, Wilfred Boggins. He smiled, leaned back in his leather chair, tapped the fingers of his hands together and smirked.

"Times up." Poole ushered Cloverfield and his notes out the door and dimmed the lights. He locked the door and sat at the desk. He would keep watch until another part-time deputy, Thomas Swan, relieved him around midnight.

CHAPTER 14

Citizens woke up to the Rocksprings Rag, and Hammond was ecstatic.

Merle Overall, a lifer of the small town, read the first paragraph for the third time.

"The night before last, on a sultry summer night a stranger rode to town. It is unclear from where he originated, or of his true intention, yet some facts may be discerned. The lights of the Western Palace shone like a beacon to a lonely traveler, and that is indeed what he appeared to be. The laughter enticed him, and the music invited him to partake in the sinful pleasures that the Palace prides itself upon, whiskey, gambling, and women. He imbibed in liquor, a little too much. His thirst quenched he sought the comfort of a 'soiled dove'."

Old Man Dabrille was aghast. Such lewd and salacious writing had never graced the pages of the Rag in all his known days. Phrases such as *'the wanton hussy,'* and *'the bleeding fists of the stranger,'* questioned his senses. He scrunched the Rag up and threw it in the fire. He immediately regretted it and bought another copy.

In the two cafes that edged either side of the main street, and in the Palace voices wagged. They were condemning, yet the people who uttered these condemnations in public were intrigued and wanted to hear more. The story was complete fiction, and controversial. They wanted more. They wanted detail. They gossiped. They cursed. More copies were bought, and Johns was woken up to print more.

Meanwhile Mrs. Overall read the final chapter.

"It was a brutal death. Blood covered the attackers' fists. His clothes were drenched in the crimson liquid. The witnesses scrambled to help, but were unsuccessful, and then when they thought all hope was lost a man stepped out of the darkness. It was the same man who had sworn to protect them. His name is Sheriff Otis Wells."

The article was an elaborate recount of a brutal affair. Phrases such as the *'twirling Dervishes,' 'he crossed the line of decency,'* and *'on the eve of a crippled morning'* littered the article. People came out to the street, they met their neighbors by the fence, and in ale and coffee houses they discussed the article. With all such works of fact and fiction the truth was hard to discern. The residents of Rocksprings were intrigued.

Hammond had dispensed with convention. He had thrown caution to the wind. He had it fixed in his mind that the citizens were boring. As a result, he took it upon himself to rouse their idle tensions. Their simple and contented life needed to be challenged. It was a long night, and he was weary. He moved into the back room and laid down on an old mattress that was on the floor. While the town bubbled along, the gossip whispered, and the intrigue sang.

Noble was sitting on the bunk reading the bible.

CHAPTER 15

Deadeye Dave and Festus Rasmussen sat around the fire. Silence embraced them and anger enticed them. They were veterans of the war and found town life difficult to manage. They preferred the quiet life. Meager of possessions and limited in their capacity to pay for supplies they, like their dead friend Jake Jenkins, often turned their hand to petty crime to survive. Deadeye claimed to be a sniper in the Civil War with over a hundred kills. It was an achievement he was proud of, but he never explained in detail the nature of the events surrounding his time in the war. Rasmussen was also silent about such gatherings. The locals had them pinned for a bunch of no-good drifters, but the troublesome spur of misery and death left their mark on the men and there was little attempt to understand their experiences. It was Festus who broke the silence.

"What do you suppose we do?"

The words hung in the air and demanded to be answered, but Deadeye was formulating a plan and now wasn't the time to speak. Rasmussen waited. He was patient when it came to his friends. Shared experiences in misery bound people closer together. His question would be answered, but in due time. They often spent long moments in silence. Whether it was in work, leisure, or thievery - little needed to be said. There were no gaps that needed to be filled with senseless chatter. They managed their memories and thoughts as best they could, and though talk was a welcome distraction at times it was a nuisance.

Deadeye looked thoughtfully into the fire. The sleek lines of the flames curved their way to the sky. A tapestry of distant memories and feelings swamped him like a warm embrace. They tangled themselves in knots and buried themselves in his chest. He felt tears welling behind his distrustful eyes. He felt the anger burn his chest. He swallowed hard and breathed deeply. It was only when he buried the memories deep down that he responded. "We can't let it slide, I know that, but we also can't go riding into town throwing our weight around. The law always wins."

"You can say that again." They had been on the wrong side of the law a few times and had spent time in the pen. That was where they met. Rasmussen, spoiling for a fight, came to Deadeye's assistance when he was being ganged up on in the yard. When the dust of the melee settled three men lay unconscious while the big man stood like the mast of a proud ship. A friendship was born. From that moment on Deadeye was treated like a king, even though it was Rasmussen who was the hero. Upon release they just happened to run into Jake, and they hit it off. Jake brought them back to town and they went into business together.

Deadeye moved to the fire and held out his hands to warm them. "I have an idea."

Festus was mule-headed and slow. He was brutal with his fists and much like Wilson Poole, the lawman, he was good at following instructions. Deadeye picked up a stick and began discussing his plan. Rasmussen smiled and guffawed. He rubbed his hands together in anticipation. When Deadeye finished talking, Festus stoked the fire. Despite their ramshackle abode they preferred the open sky to the confines of the four walls. They wrapped themselves in their blankets and stared at the stars that littered the sky. They soon became lost in their thoughts.

CHAPTER 16

Cletus Cloverfield supplied his friend Miles Hammond with the required information of his client's past and together they formulated a plan. The plan would see them both profit from the arrangement. CC would receive a percentage of the profits, while Hammond could write the salacious and sensational pieces, he would soon become known for. Hammond was disliked anyway so he reasoned that he may as well give the folks a real reason to hate him. Hammond was pretentious and expected others to fawn over him. He overestimated his importance in the lives of the citizens of Rocksprings. He desired status and wealth and as of middle age he failed to do either. His father despised the man he had become and hadn't spoken or written to him in years. Hammond was vain and laced with contempt. He possessed an ego that demanded and expected a certain level of respect and honor due him. So, when the second article was released a few days after the first and sales exceeded expectations, he felt quite smug and self-satisfied.

Mavis Williams sat at the table, sipping a cup of tea, with a dash of whiskey as she read. *"Tim Noble was born in Littlefield, Texas, to careless parents. Their mistreatment of their only child caused the boy to grow up in neglectful conditions. He was beaten and starved. Locked in a room, and isolated from those his own age. He was denied an education and grew up in social isolation. He was never taught the difference between right and wrong. Morality was a casualty of this upbringing."*

Merle Overall paced back and forth across the kitchen floor. The Rag in her hands as she read. *"How is a boy to become a man when those charged with his upbringing were not up for the challenge? The price of failure is not theirs to bear. It is Tim Nobles.' He must suffer the consequences of this neglect. He is his own teacher. His own judge. His own moral regulator. The absence of love has left an indelible scar on the heart of the accused."*

Old man Dabrille was aghast. The younger generation had grown soft. He cursed as he read the article again. He scrambled through the draw for pencil and paper and sat down at his desk to write.

Meanwhile Sheriff Otis Wells threw the Rag in the fire and vowed never to read another copy ever again. There was a reason he didn't like Hammond, and now this article justified his suspicions. He turned to the cell where Cloverfield was conversing with his client, and he interrupted their conversation. "Visiting time is up."

CC was shocked. "But we've got so much to talk about?"

"Time is up." His tone startled the lawyer, who quickly gathered his belongings, whispered to the prisoner, and gave the sheriff a wide berth as he maneuvered past him and exited the building.

His focus turned to the prisoner, and he stared coldly at him. He was about to ask him a question when the door opened. It was Walter the telegrapher.

"Afternoon, Sheriff."

Wells noticed the papers he had in his hands and beckoned for them. He sat down heavily and sighed. He swung his feet to the edge of the table and squinted as he read. After reading the documents twice he folded them and put them in his pocket. "Thanks, Walter. Have you told anybody?"

"Not a soul, Sheriff."

"Keep it that way."

Until the case would go to trial a month later, the articles kept coming.

CHAPTER 17

Judge Oliver Q. McBean was a tiresome fellow. He had given up on humanity years ago. He was once a dreamer. He believed in equality, justice, and the rule of law. That was before the reality of life cut through the seams of his ideals and left him standing alone on a sea of misery and regret. Equality was a myth, and justice, well that was the greatest lie of all. They were words, simple words with abstract meanings. It was the want and need of people to believe in the ideals of things, rather than things themselves. It was too difficult, for such idle fancies were always out of reach.

"Order in the court." He pounded the gavel half a dozen times in quick succession.

McBean didn't want to be there. He had had enough of pretending to be an upstanding citizen of Rocksprings. He liked the vices as well as anybody, it's just that like most people he could handle his consumption of those vices. Gambling, whiskey, and whores were his pleasure. Despite his age and relative infirmity, he indulged quite frequently in these pleasures.

He cast a weary and condemning gaze on the public gallery. They were silent, apart from some shuffling on the hard wooden benches that ran along either side of the back wall. They were supposed to be the law abiding and upright citizens of Rocksprings, and some of them were. Mavis Williams was an old biddy, and judgmental, but she was sitting on the bench closest to the door. Joe Denning, the banker, was on the jury along with Ned. Denning was looking respectful in his blue pin striped suit. His decor hat held delicately in his pale hands. His blubbery face was ashen and sickly.

Fools. McBean considered them all fools and liars. Firstly, they were fooling themselves that they were respectful, and secondly that they were worthy to judge the actions, qualities, and characteristics of others. He corrected himself, it is what people did, no that wasn't quite right. It's what people had to do, whether they knew it or not. The justice system was no better. It was corrupt. Why? Because people were corruptible. It was that simple.

To his right was the prosecution. Maxwell Purcell stood facing him. His hands behind his back. A smug look on his face. Clean shaven. A long thin nose, and a wide mouth. He met the man once before. Didn't like him then, doubted that he ever would. That was the sum of McBean. One chance. That's all he gave you. If you failed, then he would have nothing to do with you ever again. Sitting beside Purcell was that ugly bugger, Boggins. He was capable, McBean knew that much. He knew in an instant who to trust and who to discard.

To his left was the defense. The large man who was standing with his hands resting on his large stomach he knew well. He was a sinner. A complainer, a conniver, a fool. He had no time for Cletus Cloverfield. McBean was the only person to know about the lawyer's past. If the town folks knew they'd run him out of town. He had used this knowledge to seek favors from Cloverfield before, and the lawyer was always anxious in his presence.

"If it pleases Your Honor." Purcell couldn't stand the silence any longer, but his rehearsed speech was cut short.

"Your interruption of the court does not please me, Mr. Purcell. Sit down."

There was some laughter from the public gallery, until the judge's gruff voice warned them. "I will remove all dissenters from the public gallery. This is your warning; you have no chances." They fell silent.

"Today's proceedings are a mere preliminary hearing to establish the accused plea. Once that has been established the court will hear motions for and or against bail. If either the prosecution or the defense strays outside of that intention, then there will be cause for me to act. You have been duly warned. Therefore, you are prepared."

CHAPTER 18

His voice was gruff, and tired. "Mr. Cloverfield, instruct your client to stand."

Cloverfield whispered gently and urged Noble to stand.

McBean watched him curiously. His first impression is that the man was nothing more than an overgrown child. He didn't appear intelligent enough to rub two sticks together. He looked tired and worn out, but if McBean was right then at the end of the trial he would be exhausted.

"How do you plead?"

"Mr. Tim Noble." Cloverfield's voice echoed off the walls of the courtroom, but McBean was louder and when he interrupted him an air of seriousness fell upon the court.

"Was I talking to you?"

CC was flabbergasted. "Your Honor."

"Mr. Cloverfield, if I wanted to talk to you, I would address you in accordance with the generic yet unstated rules of polite conversation." The gallery laughed and even Purcell took delight in this rebuke. McBean pounded the gavel again, unnecessarily loud and for too long.

"Can your client speak?"

The lawyer was gob smacked and took some time to respond. Yet before he could formulate the right words, the judge unleashed again.

"Mr. Cloverfield, I suspect that this is going to be a long and drawn-out case. Doubly so if it takes you an age to respond to such simple questions. For your benefit and for those who have forgotten the question, I'll ask it again. Can your client speak?"

He answered instantly. "Yes."

McBean cast a glance across to the prosecutor. "Mr. Purcell."

"Yes, Your Honor."

"Listen carefully."

Purcell stood as stiff as a board. "Yes, Your Honor." Purcell was a wimp, but he knew his place and had respect for the court.

"I don't expect to wait for a reply over such a simple legal matter. If neither of you can tend to the affairs of the court and if the role on which you have committed, then now is your opportunity to recede your current title." He eyed them both casually, yet with a venom to poison steel. "Is that understood?"

Purcell was the first to respond. "Yes, Your Honor."

Cloverfield cursed Purcell before continuing. "Yep."

"Mr. Cloverfield, do you understand?"

He snapped to attention. "Yes, sir." His tone was clear, and his tongue was sharp.

"Now, Mr. Noble, how do you plead?"

The accused looked from his lawyer and back to the judge. His lawyer urged him to speak to avoid the wrath of McBean descending upon him.

"Not guilty."

Gasps littered the public gallery. He was cursed and condemned, as there were few who felt sorry for the killer. The reporter and the lawyer's plans had backfired. Their month-long campaign to make Noble out to be the victim had been undone.

"Is that right?" McBean's voice was level. He expected as much, and he knew what was coming next.

"By reason of insanity," added Cloverfield.

Now, the public gallery couldn't contain their outrage. They cussed and accused Cloverfield and Hammond of conspiracy. They pointed their fingers at anyone who moved. They wanted a simple conclusion to the trial. They demanded the accused to admit his fault, confess his sins. That way the good citizens of Rocksprings could put this awful tragedy behind them and forget it ever happened.

The gavel pounded, but the repeated bangs of wood on wood had no impact. Instead McBean yelled at the bailiff to clear the court.

CHAPTER 19

Hammond had a field day at his friend's expense. The esteemed Cletus Cloverfield was not impressed. He read the prompt for the article that would grace the front page of the Rag the following morning. It has been a month since the death of Jake Jenkins, and the town had had enough of Hammond's salacious reporting and gossip mongering. Still, sales were as high as when the saga began. The citizens despised Hammond yet were drawn to his every word. He was their insight into another world. They loved his turn of phrase. They admired his tenacity and courage to challenge convention. His language was contemporary, which reflected the progression of the times. This was reflected in the art and music that pushed the boundaries. Life was changing and Hammond believed people needed to get with the program. There was money to be made and he wanted as much of it as possible.

"Can't you change the story? You make me look like a fool."

Hammond smiled. "You mean McBean made you look like a fool."

The lawyer couldn't argue with that. "Why did they have to appoint that old codger to hear the case?"

Hammond felt a little sorry for his friend, but that doesn't mean he was going to change the story. "Can't change the story. Most of the town was there. Everyone knew what happened."

Cloverfield knocked back his whisky and hastily poured another. "Can't or won't?"

"Both."

Now that the air had been cleared, they sat in silence a little longer. It was Hammond who broke the silence. "So, what happens now?"

The lawyer was frustrated. He was still smarting from the series of events that transpired hours earlier. "The day after tomorrow, the trial begins. There will be opening statements and then the prosecution will call witnesses. I'll cross examine and then it'll be the defense's turn to present their case."

"Who are the witnesses for the prosecution?"

CC put on his scarf and his gloves. He ignored the question. Hammond was fishing for information. He had work to do. He would spend the time he had left going over the witness statements and working out cross examination questions. He also needed to prepare questions and answers for the doctor he found willing to support his client's insanity defense.

He left the warm office behind him. The time since the death of Jenkins had passed quickly. In this time, he had bled his client dry of his life story. He had rewritten it and with the assistance of the editor and sold the story to the folks of Rocksprings. There was some initial success in generating public sympathy for his client, but an open letter written by a Mr. William Dabrille, and published, against his advice, turned the tide against them. The public had become tired of excuses. They wanted the trial to be over with. A date for the trial was set within the first week. Purcell alighted from the stage the following week and the drama began. The town was a hive of activity. The courthouse on the edge of town was seconded by the prosecution team of Purcell and Boggins. Their regular guests included the star witness

Doris, whose last name became known as Delaware Ahoy. The two other witnesses were the man with the cigar, Josh Tomas, and the man who tried in vain to remove Noble from Jenkins' lifeless body. His name was Dwight Fotheringham.

The night air cooled his body and repelled the sweat that had beaded on the surface of his forehead in the confines of the reporter's room. Exertion of any sort troubled him, and he was feeling the pressure. McBean had scalded him. Hammond had taunted him, but he would get his revenge.

The town had gone to sleep. Barely a light flickered. He could smell the smoke and it reminded him of home when he was a child. He was lost in his thoughts, and passed down an alley before he felt a strange sensation. He turned as a man stepped out into the mouth of the alley. Sensing danger he turned back around, but he didn't quite make it before he was struck with a heavy object. He fell against the wall of the store and tried to right himself, but he was struck again. He collapsed heavily. His body thudded against the ground. He tried to open his eyes and was struck again. He was kicked in the ribs and slapped about the face.

He pleaded for his life. "Please don't kill me."

He felt his pockets being pilfered, and his wallet removed. The scarf was tightened around his throat and for a moment he thought he was going to be strangled, but the attacker released his grip, and then there was silence. He didn't hear them scurry away, but when he opened his eyes, he was alone. He leaned against the wall to regain his senses. It took him a moment to collect his thoughts, and then he scurried to his feet and went in search of the sheriff.

CHAPTER 20

Light streamed through the wide window into a spacious room. The lawyer would usually sit with his face to the window and bask in the sun while he worked earnestly. This morning, he had the curtains drawn and an extra lamp bought in so he could work in the dim space. The beating he had received the night before had shaken him. He sported a black eye, a cut lip, and a few scratches on his face. He had received worse in the past, but that wasn't on his mind. He shuffled through the witness statements, and moved some papers around on his desk, until he found a copy of Dabrille's letter to the Rocksprings Rag. He picked it up and skimmed through it.

To the Editor of the Rocksprings Rag, Miles Hammond

I am writing in response to a series of articles written by yourself and published in the Rocksprings Rag on a series of dates, since the 11th of February 1888. As a citizen of Rocksprings, it is my duty to remind you, and those that feel swayed to believe otherwise, of the responsibility of citizenship. As a proud Texan I stand shoulder to shoulder not only with my fellow Texans, but with all Americans, in proclaiming that history reflects the finest and yet not so finest examples of humanity. Citizenship is reflected in the national identity of the American. It does not merely consist of the rights we possess and/or, the pursuit of happiness, economic prosperity, if one chooses, and the pursuit of the American dream. No sir, it is much more profound than that, yet it is easy to understand. It is called responsibility.

Freedom of speech is essential, and in a healthy democratic society debate is encouraged, not sanctioned. You sir, even have the license to express your beliefs. Thus doing, the motivations for your beliefs may also be questioned, as you and the readers of this article may question mine. In the article titled, 'The Lost Son,' you refer to Luke 15: 11 - 32, otherwise known as the Parable of the Lost Son. It is here you make references to the accused, 'like a lost sheep on the plains, alone and afraid. Nothing but sorrow behind him and a bleak future ahead.' Your words, not mine. You tempt the reader to feel sorry for the accused, and the eloquence of your words pursues this aim further.

You present his childhood as a neglectful upbringing. One in which the child was abused by both parents. Of course, you provide no proof for these bold statements, except the wandering statements of the accused and of a third party, who for legal reasons shall not be named. Is it true that you did not interview the accused? I will extend this further by asking, have you ever interviewed the accused? Reliable reporting does not rely on hearsay. One establishes facts and reports the manner of those facts, as is the unwritten responsibility of your profession. In the article titled, 'Is Society to Blame?' you once again make a biblical reference, yet you do so in err. In doing so you reference Hebrews 11:10, 'for he was looking for the city which has foundations, whose architect and builder is God.' Then one could, and many have asked, then why was the accused in an establishment of ill-repute, seeking the company of whiskey and whores? This and many other topics you conveniently ignore. Instead of facts you rely on third party accounts of the accused life, which as it must, lends itself to rumor, gossip, and innuendo. I have strayed from the original purpose of my correspondence, and I apologize to the reader.

When does one assume the responsibility of their choices and the subsequent consequences, good and bad, of those choices? The case you refer to contends that a man of twenty-five was not aware of the consequences of their actions because they were raised imperfectly. If that is the measurement of morality, then I put it to you that none of us are responsible. At twenty-five men and women not only have an obligation to themselves, but also to others. They know the differences between right and wrong. They choose to act and must bear the consequences of these actions.

The citizens of Rocksprings are not fools. They are hardworking and dedicated to law and order. They rise with the sun, and rest at night. They contribute to the worth of themselves by contributing to the worth of their community. They obey the law. They are active and informed citizens, gossips, but they care for their neighbor. When Mrs. Wright broke her hip, the people rallied to support her. When the Thornton twins lost their parents, the citizens came together to nurture and provide care for them. When a storm rattled its destructive path through town, destroying windows and sending roofs into the air, the fine folks of Rocksprings, who you label backward and afraid of change, came to the rescue. Need I remind you that your premises were most severely damaged by the storm. Who was there to lend a helping hand?

The sense of community, developing and maintaining a sense of belonging are a small part of being a responsible citizen. I dare to add, because I believe it so profoundly, that engaging in the democratic process is also essential to citizenship. You, sir, neglect these qualities of the fine folks that call Rocksprings home. You condescend to them, your readers, your customers. You lecture them and think for them. But it is a grave error to assume. That is unless one assumes responsibility and accountability, which you seem reluctant to do. Your words antagonize. They scorn. They belittle. You mock and ridicule. You seem content to paint the picture of life as it should be, for everyone else but you.

The law is an extension of and represents the society that gives it its life. It reminds us, in a reasonable and just manner of our obligation to one another. A sorrowful and pitiful situation it would be if people were to expect to benefit from the opportunities provided by the law yet deem others unworthy of the same inherent dignity and quality. No, sir. You have erred. I am not to blame for your actions, as you are not to blame for mine. The victim is not to blame. Nor is society to blame. Thus, being said, no-one is to blame for the actions of the accused, except the accused. Errors in judgment occur, yet they are our errors. They do not belong to others. We cannot erase them, and pretend they never existed. Accept them, apologize, and suffer the consequences of your actions. I will leave you with a quote from Proverbs 28:4 which epitomizes the need for the law to intervene and punish those that seek to sin in the most heinous manner. 'They that forsake the law, praise the wicked.'

The lawyer scrunched up the piece of paper and threw it at the wastepaper basket in the northeastern corner of the room. It bounced off the wall and hit the floor. Feeling sorry for himself, he removed a bottle of whiskey from the bottom draw of his desk, popped the cork and took a long swig.

89

CHAPTER 21

The sheriff was reading the lawyer's statement of the beating and robbery the night before. He had nothing to work with. He went to the scene of the crime twice, once with Deputy Poole, to search but there was just no evidence. Cloverfield could not give a meaningful description of his attackers, except to say that one was thin, and one was wide. It could have been a random attack. There was evidence to support this assumption. There were no threats made against him, besides his wallet was stolen. His assailants didn't speak, so he couldn't say anything else about them. Then again, the attack could have been targeted. This was mere speculation, yet the inference had to be made that he was attacked because of his involvement in the current case. It could have been someone with a grudge, or as the evidence suggests a random attack of opportunity. Either way he needed to take precautions. He was pondering on such thoughts when the bell on the door sounded, and deputies Poole and Swan entered.

It was the laconic voice of Swan that spoke. "You wanted to see us, Sheriff.'

Poole sat on the chair opposite the sheriff while Swan, leaning a little to the left, stood with a Henry rifle in his right hand, and a customary six gun on his right hip.

"The attack on CC has got me thinking."

"Any progress, Otis?"

"Nothing to go on, but it's best we play it safe. Could be a random attack or related to the case. That means we keep a vigil on CC and the prisoner."

Swan spoke. "We haven't seen or heard of Jake's partners. They didn't even go to his funeral. Do you think it could be some type of revenge attack?"

Poole added. "They couldn't get to the prisoner, so the next best thing is the man that represents him."

Wells nodded. "Everything you say makes sense. We're taking no chances. I've asked CC if he wants a guard."

Both men interrupted by laughing yet it was Poole who responded and spoke for both. "Sorry about that, Sheriff. I can just hear CC blowing off steam."

Wells chuffed. "You're right of course, he gave me an earful and refused any assistance. Still, the offer was made and though it was rejected we have a responsibility to the prisoner, and that's why you are here."

"What do you want us to do?"

"It's getting late. Stay here with the prisoner and take turns resting. Tomorrow the trial begins, and I've got a feeling you are going to need your rest. I'll be here before eight. Trial begins at ten, so we'll have time to make sure everything is fine."

"I've been thinking about the whole situation, Sheriff."

He watched the deputy scratch his chin. "What's on your mind?"

"If someone wanted to kill CC, they could have done that right easily. Instead, they were sending him a message."

"I've considered the proposition and there's only a couple of people that would have the gall to try such a thing."

"Deadeye and Festus." Swan responded.

"They've been quiet since their partner's killing. Haven't seen them in town." Added Poole.

Wells mused. "Had no need to warn them, until now."

Swan shifted his weight. "What do you suppose we do?"

Wells stood and paced back and forth. The deputies had never seen him this on edge before. "That courthouse is built too far away. They should have moved the jailhouse closer, as I suggested when I assumed office."

Poole spoke determinedly. "I know the boys well enough. Do you want me to talk to them? I could leave in the morning and be back by late afternoon."

Wells stopped before the men. "It's best if I maintain control in town, besides, I could be called to give evidence. We'll get Noble to court safely and then you'll have to ride out. Thomas and I will guard the prisoner at the courthouse. If there is an inclination that trouble is brewing, we'll wait for your return before transporting the prisoner."

Thirty minutes later Poole had a range of questions he would ask the men, scribbled on a piece of paper. He folded this and put it in his pocket. The sheriff yawned and rubbed his eyes. "It's going to be a big day tomorrow. Get some rest."

Wells stood to leave. "I'll check on CC and then go home."

"Rest easy, Otis."

The deputies were glad that Wells was the sheriff. He was steady and reliable. He dealt with things as they occurred, and straight down the line. There was the law, and though he didn't always agree with it, he tended to it like a mother to a sick child. The man couldn't lie even if he wanted to. He was a pious man and though Swan couldn't commit to such a life he was wise enough to know a good man when he met one, and Wells was it.

"Get some rest Wilson. I'll stand guard." Poole didn't argue. He found a spot on the floor beneath the bench and was quickly snoring.

Swan turned down the oil lamp. The smokey remnants of the wick filled the air. The room was dark, and silent. The street was almost deserted. A tired lawman turned the corner and from a block away he could see a light emanating from the lawyer's abode.

Burning the midnight oil in preparation for the biggest case of his life.

95

CHAPTER 22

Wells knocked on the door for the third time. No response again. He grasped the door handle and turned the knob. It was open and he let himself in. He removed his single-action colt from the faded leather holster and cocked the trigger. He stepped lightly for a big man, breathing deeply. His senses were on high alert. He felt the silence. He heard his heart thudding in his chest. He heard a crash coming from what he knew as the lawyer's office. His strides lengthened and quickened.

"This is the sheriff. Step through the door with your hands up."

Not a sound. Without pausing he kicked the door in, and it slammed against something heavy and came back at him. He saw the body of the lawyer lying on the floor. Sensing that danger had passed he stepped inside and that's when the reality of what had transpired hit him. Cloverfield was dead. Dead drunk. An empty bottle of brandy lay on its side beside his prone figure while another sat on top of his large oak desk. It was then that Wells heard the snoring. He holstered and shook his head in disgust. What was the man thinking? He was twelve hours away from the most important case of his life and he lay in a drunken stupor. Wells had little sympathy for self-inflicted misery.

He went to the end of the small hallway, opened the back door, and pumped a bucket of water from the well in the backyard. He proceeded to throw it carelessly on the big man, but the cold rush of the water barely startled him. He retrieved another bucket and poured it slowly and purposely on his face. Cloverfield spluttered and cussed. He tried to sit but could only manage crawling over onto his knees.

He emanated a low and gruff groan. It was obvious that he was too intoxicated to function. He tried to speak, but the words came out in a jumbled mess. Swaying not so majestically he fell face first to the floor. By this time Wells had returned with another bucket of water. He rolled the man over, ripped the buttons of his shirt as he nearly tore it off his chest. Pouring the water over his torso, he threw the bucket on the floor near the jumbled mess of scrunched up paper that had failed to find its mark.

Intoxication was a sin. If men spent as much time avoiding sin as they did indulge in it, they would be better off. Wells was strait-laced and determined in this regard. He knew the type of man he wanted to be, and that didn't include salacious lubrication of the evil spirits. Locking the back door, he moved to the front door, and pulled it closed behind him.

The evening was cool and breezy. He had worked up a temper. He hated it when others boiled his blood. He felt hot and sweaty. The lawyer had irked him, and without even trying. He understood Cloverfield's frustrations. He was shown up in court by a surly judge well past retirement, yet with the intellectual quip to whip lash anyone that rebuked his care. He also knew about the article that was to be published the following morning. Such sleights to his reputation, or what was left of it, caused him some angst. Add the assault to his person and the extraction of his belongings and a man might turn to drink to ponder, perhaps not on the meaning of life, but at least the current course of action.

He would leave him to sober up on his own accord. He is no man's keeper. If he failed to appear in court, it would be of his doing. He considered the article written by Dabrille a few weeks ago now. What was it that he said?

He did the buttons of his coat up as he tried to recall Dabrille's essential message. Responsibility, that was it. People were responsible, thus accountable. It was that simple. Straying from this premise opened the door that could never be closed again.

CHAPTER 23

The courtroom was silent. Everyone was ready. Judge McBean sat staring out across the packed room. Purcell the prosecutor fidgeted. He looked over his shoulder at the door every thirty seconds, hoping that it would swing open, and the larger-than-life Cletus Cloverfield would enter. He was eager to begin the trial. Everyone was waiting. The jury were in position. They sat motionless staring at the door. The prisoner was in the dock, Swan standing next to him. Noble's feet were shackled to the floor and his arms were fastened to the hook jutting out from the side of the cubicle in which he sat. Swan was a tall and handsome man. Short brown hair, clean shaven. He looked serious, but that was typical. He was a good deputy when needed. When he wasn't playing lawman, he ran his mother's small ranch a few miles from town.

Miles Hammond removed a watch from his pocket for the second time in a minute. He was anticipating an interesting day in court and had writing paper and several pencils. He looked dapper in his dark suit. As one observer noted when they entered the public gallery an hour earlier. He looked like a man with money.

In the jury dock, the store owner, Ned, was squished in next to the banker, Joe Denning. In the public gallery Merle Overall was positioned delicately at the end of the bench closest to the door, as was Walter the telegrapher. The public gallery was full, and those that attended the trial for the duration sat in the same place's day after day. Sitting in front of Mrs. Overall was Millie Tippet. Miss Tippet was a shy and awkward creature. Cruelly considered the local spinster. She had been the subject of much gossip and rumor over the years at the hands of Mavis Williams and the woman who sat behind her. Tippet's presence shocked most people, as she was quite the recluse, so to see her in the courthouse surprised several of the locals. Little did they know that Hammond's portrayal of the accused touched her heart. She felt isolated and alone just like Noble. Her upbringing at the hands of an unruly and uncaring mother had shaped how she responded to people. She was not there out of a sense of duty, as Dabrille would like to think. She was drawn to the accused, and it was

Hammond who made it happen. Millie Tippet was in love, and it was only she who knew it.

"Sheriff, please approach the bench." Wells did as was instructed by the judge. Members of the public gallery strained to hear the conversation yet only heard the neutered whispers of a frustrated judicial official.

"Go and find that lawyer and bring him here at once."

"I can't do that, Your Honor."

Now McBean was angry. "Why not?"

"I am needed here. As I told you before, the prisoner's life may be in danger."

"Well, where's Poole?"

"Out of town on an errand."

Light streamed in through the high windows. It was a little after ten-thirty. A fly buzzed, and people began to sweat. It was unusually hot for this time of year. The sound of restlessness began to stir the crowd. There were a few mumbles of dissatisfaction. McBean picked up the gavel, sat up straight and was about to adjourn court when the door flew open and a ragged and out of breath Cloverfield entered the room. His appearance was disheveled. His clothes wrinkled and his tie was mismatched and askew. He pushed through the swing gates that separated the public gallery from the forecourt and moved across to his table.

His words were thick because his mouth was dry. "Apologies for the disruption to the proceedings, Your Honor."

McBean leaned forward and tapped the gavel gently. "Court adjourned for one hour. I will see both lawyers in my chambers."

There were rumblings of discontent. The court cleared and the prisoner was removed and escorted to a private room at the back of the courthouse. In two minutes, the room was deserted.

CHAPTER 24

"What do you have to say for yourself?" McBean was measured, but furious. He had no time for incompetence and tolerated none in his courtroom.

"Water, I need water."

As a sign of goodwill Purcell's assistant, Wilfred Boggins, left the room and returned a few minutes later with a pitcher of water and a dirty glass.

CC drank heartily, gulped, and then drank again. Draining the pitcher in no time at all. He sighed, wiped his hand across his mouth and tried to address the judge.

"I. Um, I."

Before he could find an excuse McBean spoke. "You smell like whiskey. Don't even try to defend yourself."

Purcell interrupted. Like a hungry lion he had sensed a wounded gazelle and he moved in for the kill. "The state is ready to proceed with the trial, Your Honor. We would request the trial begin immediately."

He waved Purcell's request away. "We will resume in a little under an hour."

McBean resumed his lecture. "This is a high-profile case, Mr. Cloverfield. It is in your best interests to carry yourself with a certain decorum that is fit for the title you carry. You do know that your client can deem you incompetent and request another lawyer."

"You cannot be serious."

"I am, Mr. Cloverfield, and I'm just in the right mind to dismiss you myself for incompetence."

Purcell interrupted. "You can't be talking about a mistrial. Your Honor, I object."

"McBean laughed. This is not a courtroom, Purcell. There will be no mistrial. This case will be heard, for it's in the public's interest to do so. What I won't do is subject the public, most importantly my court to the incompetencies of counsel." His voice rose and his quips were sharp.

"The defense and prosecution will be early, and they will be prepared. If I notice one more act of incompetence that has the potential to influence the outcome of this case, I will report you to the bar. Are we understood?"

Cloverfield was sheepish. His head hurt and he needed to go to the toilet. He was tired and his voice was weak. "Yes, Your Honor."

The room was quiet. Everyone was waiting for the judge to speak and when he did his words took Purcell and Boggins by surprise. His voice was harsh. "Mr. Purcell and Mr. Boggins, do you understand what I am saying?"

Boggins' mouth fell open, and he looked at the lead prosecutor who stared at the judge. Purcell was seething. He was not in err here. Cloverfield had tested the patience of the court and had been reprimanded. On the other hand, the prosecution had always acted professional. The rebuke was unjustified. Purcell was not so easily intimidated. He was wispy and smart, but no candle flame. "I would like it noted," he said in a calm and measured tone as he looked from the judge to the stenographer patiently scribbling away in the corner of the room, and then back to the judge, "that I object to your rebuke of the prosecution."

"You can protest all you like, Purcell. I am waiting for a response."

Boggins just wanted to agree so the tense standoff could end, but Purcell persisted. He was polite, and cunning. He could use this rebuke as a means of appeal if the case didn't work out the way he anticipated. He figured that he had to get McBean on record with some form of commitment. The cogs were turning fast and as always, he found a method of doing just that. "Is the prosecution in error?"

"Mr. Purcell, you try my patience."

"What is the cause of the prosecution's rebuke?"

McBean was seething, but he kept his voice measured. "Mr. Purcell, I am merely establishing the expectations of the court."

"I am aware of the professional standards and expectations of court operations, and of my role and responsibility as the prosecution. On the other hand, the accused defense counsel is a little vague about his ethical responsibility."

Cloverfield was too annoyed with himself to argue the point.

Purcell persisted. "What has been the cause of the rebuke of the prosecution?"

McBean had been forced into a corner. Purcell was right. The judge could either admit the prosecution had done nothing to warrant such a tongue lashing or he could ignore it altogether. Purcell had a reputation as playing everything by the rules and being a dogged and determined adversary. Besides, he had political connections. He had two choices, push the issue, and or apologize. He would do neither. Instead, he replied, "court will resume in thirty minutes."

CHAPTER 25

"Your Honor, gentlemen of the jury and the distinguished citizens of Rocksprings."

"Mr. Purcell, you will address the court, and the court only."

He smiled mischievously at the judge, but there was no hint of antagonism in his voice, "yes, Your Honor. I apologize. It will not happen again."

A message had been sent and received. He continued. "The prosecution, on the behalf of the state of Texas, have sufficient, no, overwhelming evidence that the accused, Tim Noble, did willfully, criminally, and sanely murder one, Mr. Jake Jenkins. Witnesses will be called to give evidence as to the nature of the offense committed and the extent of the attack of the accused on the deceased."

Millie Tippet heard the confident and determined voice of Purcell and admired his tenacity, but her focus was on the defendant. She admired his pale yet flushed skin. His eyes looked innocent. The man was out of place. He didn't belong here. Not like this. He was too innocent. She believed Hammond' spin. Goaded beyond endurance. Twenty-five years of torment and ridicule had come to an end. She had learned from the experience how the pain of words shapes a person's outlook on themselves and others. Her mother who died five years earlier was an esteemed pillar of the Rocksprings community. Privately she was nasty and spiteful. She ridiculed, cursed, and despised her daughter with words, and for as long as she could remember she had backed these up with threats of physical violence. When her mother took sick and died, she cried, not for the loss of her mother for the misery she had left behind.

She considered Noble delicately. She admired his large eyes, like saucers. They stared off into the distance, fearful and unsure. She shed a tear and wiped it away with one of her mother's handkerchiefs. Purcell continued to lecture the court.

"It will be proven beyond a reasonable doubt that the accused, one Tim Noble, did commit murder on that balmy night right out there." He pointed for effect. "In your main street. A man was beaten to death by HIM." He pointed at the accused. Purcell commanded the center floor of the court as he continued his speech to the jury. "When the arguments in this case have closed, and all submissions to the evidence have been presented you will have no option. I said NO option, but to find the defendant GUILTY of murder."

Millie returned her focus to the man in the cubicle. Then suddenly, her heart skipped a beat when he looked at her and for a moment their eyes met. She smiled at him, and thus returning her gesture a bond was sealed.

The prosecutor marched across the floor, like an experienced actor citing Shakespeare. Confident and theatrical. His voice rising and falling. It was a rehearsed speech. Cloverfield straightened his tie and gulped nervously. McBean looked at his watch. There was strictly no time limit on opening and or closing addresses, so long as they didn't stray outside the purview of their intention, and Purcell had managed it well.

"Thank you, Your Honor."

McBean smiled. "Thank you, Mr. Purcell. Will the defense make their opening statement now or will they defer until their defense?"

Not himself. Cloverfield started to speak while sitting and then corrected himself. He stood and in a loud voice said, "the defense will defer, Your Honor."

"Excellent. Mr. Purcell you may call your first witness."

Millie and the accused continued to stare at one another, oblivious to the proceedings of the court.

Purcell snapped to attention. "The prosecution calls Miss. Ahoy."

CHAPTER 26

"Please state your name for the court."

"My name is Doris Delaware Ahoy."

"What is your occupation?"

"WHORE." The public gallery broke out into laughter. The comment threatened to derail the swift proceeding to the trial. McBean needed to make a stand and he did.

"Bailiff," he pointed his gavel at Peter Thorpe, a local rapscallion, and said, "remove that man from my court."

Thorpe tried to protest but thought better of it when Sheriff Wells tapped him on the shoulder and hitched his thumb to the door. The crowd quietened down instantly. "Any more outbursts like that and I will close the public gallery."

The judge addressed the witness. "I apologize for the intrusion. Please answer Mr. Purcell's question."

She looked unsure and went quite red with embarrassment. "I. Ah. I am a hostess."

Purcell shuffled forward and spread his arms in a warm gesture. "Your morality is not on trial, Miss. Ahoy, please answer the question."

She resigned herself to her fate. She had to answer the question. "A whore."

"Is the man who murdered Jake Jenkins in this courtroom today?"

"Objection Your Honor."

"On what ground, Mr. Cloverfield?"

"On the insinuation that my client is a murderer."

McBean held back a smile. "What is the accused charged with?"

"Why murder of course?"

"There is a subtle distinction, Mr. Cloverfield, but it makes a world of difference. Objection sustained. You may continue Mr. Purcell, but you will rephrase the question."

"Thank you, Your Honor. I will repeat the question. Is the man who killed Jake Jenkins in this courtroom today?"

Her voice was audible, but meek. "Yes."

"Can you point him out please?"

"Objection, Your Honor. In his haste to stand the chair scraped across the floor and fell over."

"On what ground, Mr. Cloverfield?"

"Leading the witness."

McBean was testing the lawyer, but he knew the grounds were legitimate. He just wanted to know if the lawyer could explain sufficiently. "Please explain."

"The prosecution stated that the murderer is a male. That is leading."

Purcell interrupted. "Your Honor. The killer of Mr. Jenkins is not in dispute. The defense will testify to this, so why the objection?"

"Thank you, Mr. Purcell. You are right. Mr. Cloverfield sit down, and only object when you have cause to do so." Mumbled McBean.

Purcell continued. "Can you point that person out please?"

With a shaking hand and crooked finger, she pointed to the accused.

"Let the record show," crooned Purcell, "that the witness pointed to the accused, Timothy Noble."

"Duly noted. Please continue."

"When did you come into contact with the accused?"

"On the night that Jake was killed."

"Where did you meet the accused?"

"At work?"

"Where do you work, Miss. Ahoy?"

"At the Western Palace."

"How did you meet the accused?"

"Well, he was sitting at a table, near the roulette wheel, staring off into space. I sat opposite him and began a conversation."

"What was the conversation about?"

She hung her head and blushed. "Business."

"Please tell the court what happened."

The words fell out of her mouth in a rush, as if a great weight had been lifted from her shoulders. "He propositioned me, but I declined his advance. I stood to walk away, and he chased after me and pushed me over. I was being attacked. He rushed past me to the door. Jake, he was such a gentleman. He was always looking out for us ladies. You know we are not treated that well. Some clients treat us worse than cattle."

Purcell interrupted, "Miss. Ahoy, what happened next?"

"Jake helped me up off the floor. He asked what happened, and when I told him he followed him," she pointed to the accused again, "outside."

"What transpired next?"

"Pardon me."

"What happened next?"

"Jake," she started to cry on cue, "Mr. Jenkins, a noble gentleman, asked the man to apologize."

"I know this is difficult, Miss. Ahoy, but please try your best to remember what happened next."

She pointed her crooked finger at the accused again. "He," she dabbed her eyes, "challenged Mr. Jenkins and Jake had to hit him to avoid being attacked."

Doris continued to relate the series of events that led to the man's death. When she had finished her tears had dried up.

"No more questions, Your Honor. "

"Very well, Mr. Purcell."

Doris went to vacate the witness box. "Please stay seated, Miss Ahoy. You will now be cross-examined by the defense."

The lawyer stood, straightened his tie, and moved beyond his table to the center of the floor. He folded his hands behind his back. His face turned from the jury to the public gallery and back again. He moved across to the railing that separated the jury from the main floor and leaned on it. He stared at them in turn. He knew them all. Ned the store owner and Denning the banker amongst them. He had dealings with all the men, some good and still some debts unpaid. A fear swept through him that they would hold a grudge, and this would sway their verdict.

He moved back to the floor and stopped three feet in front of the witness box. "Miss. Ahoy, could you please tell the court where you were standing when the fighting started."

The poor woman sniffled. "On the top of the stairs."

Purcell instructed her to keep her responses brief. The more she said the more that could be taken out of context. Made sense to her, besides, she didn't want to talk any more than she had to.

"How far away were the men standing when they started fighting?"

"Six feet."

"And you saw everything?"

"I saw what I saw."

There were a few chuckles from the gallery.

"You said that Mr. Jenkins hit first."

"Yes."

"So, he was the aggressor?"

"No."

"But he hit first."

"The accused stepped aggressively toward him."

"Did you try to stop the fight?"

"Yes."

"What did you do?"

"Why, I said stop."

More chuckles from the gallery.

The lawyer went quiet and paced back and forth across the floor. A weary silence fell upon the room. It bordered on restlessness, but no one spoke. They saw what happened to Thorpe and didn't want the same fate.

"When the accused was straddling the deceased and he was called to stop, why do you think he didn't respond?"

"Objection, Your Honor. The witness is asked to formulate conjecture, as to the defendant's state of mind."

"What say you, Mr. Cloverfield?" McBean was hungry and it was lunch time. Besides, he could do with a nap, but he wanted to get this witness processed as soon as possible and he had to persist.

"I withdraw the question."

Another minor win for Purcell. He was even more smug than normal.

"Very well, please continue." The judge stifled a yawn.

Cloverfield moved across to his table and fiddled with some papers on his desk and found the piece of paper with the anticipated questions he started working on the day before. He drank too much and neglected his duty. He had nothing and he began to sweat.

McBean was anxious for the witness to be dismissed. "The defense may continue with their line of questioning."

Cloverfield turned toward the bench. "What was your relationship with the deceased?"

"Excuse me."

"Was he a client?"

The little lawyer sprang to his feet, "objection, on the grounds of relevance."

"Overruled. Please answer the question."

Sheepishly she muttered, "on occasion."

He turned to the jury. "I am just trying to establish the relationship between the witness and the deceased. The credibility of the witness is in question. The witness' profession has been established, therefore the moral integrity of the deceased is subject to scrutiny."

"Objection, the deceased is not on trial here." Purcell was outraged.

"Approach the bench."

The lawyer's eyed one another and approached the bench cautiously.

"Cletus, you are treading on dangerous water."

"Your Honor. It is in the public's best interest to grasp the integrity of the deceased."

"On what grounds?"

"Merely to establish his credibility and the application of this in regard to instigating the fight."

"Mr. Purcell."

"He is trying to taint the man's reputation. I repeat, Mr. Jenkins is not on trial here. May I remind Mr. Cloverfield that it is not the job of the court to prove his case."

McBean knew his response before he called them to the bench. "Your request is denied. Try a different line of questioning or sit down."

Frustrated and hung over. Tired and annoyed. Angry and sweaty. He had enough and without thinking he blurted out. "How much do you charge for entertainment?"

Before the prosecutor could object, Doris said, "you should know, I've satisfied your need on more than a few occasions."

The gallery went off. They laughed and pointed at the lawyer. They whispered to one another and the noise crew to a crescendo. Cloverfield raised his voice but was drowned out in the hubbub. Purcell sat with his arms folded across his chest and smiling like a Cheshire cat. Boggins was giggling. Millie and the accused were smiling at one another. McBean was pounding his gavel, and though no one was listening he adjourned court until the following morning.

CHAPTER 27

Deadeye took a sip of cool water from a rusty enamel mug and cast his eyes to the west. The sun was sinking. It was late afternoon. The sun was high in the sky and scorched the earth. He paused and tipped the rest of the water on his head. He started as the water ran down his back.

"Rider coming."

His partner rose from the earthen pit thirty seconds later. He was covered from head to toe in soot. He followed his partner's lead and drank heartily. "Who do you think it is?"

Deadeye responded as he moved across to the fire and threw another log on. "Sits the horse like a lawman."

Festus was nervous. Any mention of the law made his palms sweat. He promised himself that he would never go back to jail. When he was nervous, he stuttered. "Wh…what, what do you think they want?"

"You just keep your mouth shut. Let me do all the talking."

They waited in silence, but they didn't have to wait long before Poole drew rein a minute later. He was polite and obliging. "Good afternoon, mind if I alight and stretch for a while?"

"Sure, Deputy."

"In need of rain. The country is as dry as I have ever seen it."

Corking his canteen, he nodded in agreement. "Sure enough, I don't know how you manage to live out here, being so barren and dry." Poole kept hold of the saddle and moved across to the sparse shade cast by the crippled awning of the rundown hut.

"What's the meaning of your visit, Deputy?"

"Haven't seen you in town since Jake was killed."

"Is there a problem with that?" His voice was rough and edgy.

"Strange is all. Your partner gets killed and you ain't making a holler."

"Nothing to fuss about, besides I hear the law has everything under control."

"Unusual is all. The times must be changing."

"Now Deputy, you didn't ride all the way out here for that. What else is on your mind?"

"Yeah, I suppose it's written all over my face."

"Sure enough, but not in the sweet language that the reporter uses."

That piqued the deputy's interest. "You've read some of his articles?"

Deadeye pointed to the fire. "That's how we start the fire."

Festus guffawed. He looked at Deadeye who smiled and then back to the deputy. He stopped smiling and continued to stare.

"How do you get the articles if you don't go into town?"

"Travelers. More drifters than you think are trying to escape town life. There's been a few through here. Strangers mostly."

"Mostly, but not always?"

It was a great question and Deadeye reprimanded himself for talking too much. He decided to change the subject before the lawman could ask him another question. "So, what's the real reason you rode out here? It wasn't just to be civil. We're hospitable men, but we have work to do."

"Two nights ago, the lawyer of the man who is defending Jake's killer was beaten and robbed. The description of the two men describes you and Festus."

"You are figuring we're guilty of beating on some blabbermouth?"

"I ain't supposing you did anything. Asking questions is all."

"Well, it wasn't us. We were here sleeping under the stars. The same as every night."

"Is there anyone to verify your presence?"

"One another, and our word as men."

"Your word."

Deadeye smiled, stood, and stretched. "Now, I can't figure out if that is the problem with the law or lawmen."

Poole was feeling nervous. He stood before two men without a firearm, and he was almost accusing them of a crime. There were rumors of lots of petty theft that had been committed by the veterans, but no concrete evidence. They had always been on the law's radar. "What problem is that?"

"I've told you where we were. There are no witnesses to say we were here, and no witnesses to say we weren't. We were not in town. We did not beat up the blabbermouth. We've done nothing but the right thing throughout this whole ordeal, Deputy. Jake was our partner, and our friend but we have, and will continue to abide by the law. If the law delivers justice, we'll be content."

"And if justice is not served?"

"Then you'll hear from us, and justice will be carried out."

"Is that a threat?"

"Nope, it's a promise, Deputy." Deadeye had nothing else to say. He said as many words as possible in ten minutes than he had in ten years and that bothered him. "Come on Fess, let's get back to work."

They left Deputy Poole standing by their shack. He quickly mounted and made a hasty retreat from the camp.

CHAPTER 28

Wells was making notes about an incident that happened earlier that afternoon. Riley McIntosh had accused his brother Logan of stealing a mare. Despite the high-profile case there was still the law to uphold, and he wouldn't be able to do it without Poole and Swan. They were good men and when the trial was over, he would invite them into his home for dinner. The local carpenter, Bernard Wright, finished his work. Wells had got permission and the funds from the Chamber of Commerce to put solid walls on the outside of the prison bars to protect the prisoner's privacy and hide him from the increasing traffic that entered his office. He sent Swan home once they returned the prisoner safely to jail. He would be due to return for the night shift. He was just finishing off the paperwork when the door opened and Deputy Poole, looking a little ragged, entered.

"Howdy, Sheriff?"

He laid the pencil on the table, removed his glasses, and rubbed his eyes. "Wilson, relax. Coffee?"

"Sure." He sat heavily and waited as the sheriff moved about the room.

"What do you think of the renovations?"

He accepted the coffee. It scalded the palms of his hands, but it was welcome. "Wright knows his work."

"It was finished by the time we returned from court."

"Efficient too."

"How did your meeting with Deadeye and Festus go?"

"I don't mind telling you that there's a cold streak that runs right through Deadeye."

"I've heard rumors about him in the war, but he has kept his nose clean since he has been in Rocksprings. There's been suspicion of criminal behavior and as you know we have investigated certain crimes regarding that pair, but we have nothing to go on."

Poole informed the sheriff what transpired during his visit to the mine, and when he finished, he yawned.

"I know it's been a big day, but I want you to write a statement about what happened before you turn in for the night. Swan will be here soon. "I'm going for a walk around town. I'll pass by Cloverfield's residence. First, I am going to the Palace to make my presence known."

"Alright, Sheriff. I'll do as you ask, and I'll relieve Swan early in the morning."

Wells stood, picked up the Greener, and patted Poole on the shoulder as he moved past him, and through the door into the cool night air. The Palace was loud, after a lull since the death of Jenkins and with the trial, strangers, and folks from everywhere had flocked to town. Rocksprings had garnished as much attendance as the decent citizens expected and they were tired. They were tired of the noise. They were weary of the gossip yet couldn't get enough of it. Especially the daily one-page articles about the case written by the controversial figure of Miles Hammond. Dabrille had not written another letter, but the folks wanted it. They liked what he had to say. Dabrille preferred the quiet life and ventured out rarely, and only Walter knew that he had written three more letters to Hammond and none of them had been printed. Hammond changed his mind. It's okay to encourage people to challenge your viewpoint, until they do. Hammond was that type of man. It was easier to plead ignorance and that is what Hammond would do if he were ever challenged.

Wells' appearance at the Palace was normal, and he moved around the room, and conversed with the barman, Mince, before leaving. He made his way down the long main street. There were no pedestrians about, and he made his way to the lawyer's residence. Lights were on so he knocked sharply. A minute later the door opened and Cloverfield answered the door.

"Everything alright?"

"Yes, Sheriff."

Wells wanted to talk about the case, but Purcell informed him that he would be called as a witness either tomorrow or the day after, and that it wasn't in his interest to converse with anyone about the case. "Alright then. I'll move on. Just one more thing."

"Sure."

"You might want to ask who is at the door before opening it."

He smiled. "Right you are, Sheriff. Right you are."

Meanwhile, Wiley Johns held the article up in the air. He read the title and shook his head. He most certainly didn't need the money, and he had no idea why he was working for Hammond. The man was an antagonist. He knew better than to argue with or question him. Instead, he questioned his morality and continued to print the required number of copies.

CHAPTER 29

"Who do you think you are? You're supposed to be my friend." Cloverfield burst his way into Hammond' office when he read the headline of the current news article, '*Questionable Counsel Questions Questionable Witness.*'"

Hammond, smug and self-satisfied, moved across the floor to his desk, removed a cigar from the top drawer and lit it defiantly. "We are friends."

Cloverfield tore the article into shreds and let the pieces drop on the floor. "Some friend."

Hammond blew a thick cloud of smoke condescendingly in the lawyers' direction. "Quit your bellyaching. You're getting your fair share of the profits."

Cloverfield cussed and kicked the floor. "Well, I don't like being the brunt of anyone's jokes. I won't live this down."

Hammond decided it was best to win his friend over. "Alright, I'll focus on other stories from here on in."

"You better. This tripe is slanderous, and one more word from you and I will sue you for everything you've got. I'm out. You are on your own."

The lawyer left without another word. He picked up the article from his desk. He did make his business colleague look bad, but that's all it was, business. He had no deep-seated affection or respect for him. He was a means to an end, and that end was money, and fame. He didn't care what he had to print, or who he had to climb over to attain it. Just to be safe, he decided that he would focus on some other calamity of the trial. What could he write about it? Judges always had political connections and if the rumors were true Purcell could be running for governor in a few short years, so it didn't make much sense to attack those who could assist him.

The three lawmen moved the prisoner to the courthouse and while the deputies kept watch inside the sheriff went outside for some fresh air. He was feeling poorly. He had tried the usual pills and liniment, and despite his wife's protests he donned the badge and embraced the day. Despite the hour sweat beaded on his forehead. It was a sure sign the man was off color. As he sat beneath the tree out front of the courthouse a woman approached him.

"Excuse me, Sheriff Wells."

He peered through the dappled shade at the young woman, and it was a while before recognition took hold. "Miss. Tippet, good morning. The trial will begin soon. People are starting to gather. The doors will open soon."

She was obviously shy and not used to conversation. "I am about to ask you a question, Sheriff, and while it may seem odd to you, please consider my request with the seriousness of which I ask it."

He fought back the indigestion and swallowed hard. "Of course, Miss. Tippet, you have my complete respect."

She smiled awkwardly. "The prisoner, um. I. Ah. Is the accused permitted visitors at the jailhouse?"

He was shocked, but nonetheless answered her fairly. "Prisoners are permitted visitors. Visitors are not allowed in the cells and their interactions will be monitored, but yes visitors are welcomed."

She appeared to perk up at this news. "Is it okay if I visit Mr. Noble?"

It was none of his business, so he didn't ask. He just assumed. "That's noble of you Miss Tippet, no pun intended. One's Christian duty is never complete. I am sure he will appreciate your kindness."

"Thank you, Sheriff. You are so kind. Mother spoke so highly of you. A Christian man if I ever did see one, she'd say."

"Much obliged for your kindness."

"What time do you think would be best?"

"Anytime, about an hour after the proceedings are canceled for the day. Each visit is forty minutes in length and only one visit per day."

"That sounds more than fair, Sheriff. Thank you."

The doors of the courthouse opened, and it was time to leave. "Just one thing, Miss. Tippet."

"Please, call me Millie."

He nodded, "Millie, are you not worried about what the likes of Mavis Williams will say when she finds out you have visited the prisoner?"

She stood straight and with as much confidence as he had ever seen in her she responded. "As you have said, Mr. Wells, one's Christian duty is never done."

CHAPTER 30

"No more questions, Your Honor."

Jonas Tomas sat nervously in his chair. He was to be cross-examined by Cloverfield and the man didn't look happy.

The lawyer knew the eyes of the court were upon him. The article was published, and he had continued to be the whipping boy of Hammond. He heard their whispers when he walked the long main street to the courthouse, and they intensified when he entered the courtroom.

He stood hastily. Loud and clumsy. He knocked the table and spilled his glass of water. There was some laughter, but he ignored it. He didn't care. He approached the witness box in great stride.

"Mr. Tomas, do you consider yourself a good citizen?"

McBean sensed an objection but was too quick for the prosecutor. "Before you object, Mr. Purcell, I will allow the question."

"Well, Mr. Tomas, can you please answer the question?"

"I suppose so."

"Do you know if you are a good citizen or not?"

"I think so."

"Is that a, yes?"

Tomas looked from Purcell to the judge and receiving no support from either answered the question. "Yes. I am a good citizen."

"What makes a good citizen?"

"Excuse me?"

"You just admitted to being a good citizen. What makes a good citizen?"

Before the witness could respond the lawyer antagonized him with a series of questions.

"Is a good citizen arrested for being drunk and disorderly?"

"Is a good citizen one who refuses to pay their debts?"

"What about public nakedness, Mr. Tomas?"

"Well, it wasn't like that." The witness tried to respond.

"It wasn't like that. The first, second or third times?"

"You're making me seem bad."

"You're doing a good enough job on your own. But this case is not about you, Mr. Tomas, so let's turn to the night of the tragic death of Mr. Jenkins. You have just described the scene of that most horrendous night, but there are two things I would like to cover, and then you'll be free to go." He held up two fingers, one from each hand.

"Did you find the fight amusing?"

"Well, it was kind of funny at the beginning, but then it went bad really quick."

"Did you laugh at the confrontation?"

"Perhaps, I was drunk."

"Such a noble citizen, a family man, drunk late at night laughing while a man was beaten to death."

"Objection, Your Honor."

"I apologize to the court, and I withdraw the statement."

McBean grumbled, "Counsel, you are walking a tightrope."

With his arms behind his back, he bowed respectfully to the judge, and then continued.

"Please describe Mr. Noble's manner when he retaliated to Mr. Jenkins."

"He lost control. He was like a man possessed. Jake tried to defend himself, but it was like he," pointing to the accused, "had the strength of ten men. Someone called out to stop but he ignored them."

"Is it possible that he didn't hear them?"

"I suppose so. I mean he was out of his mind."

Boggins hung his head. Purcell sprang into action. "Objection."

"On what grounds?"

"Mr. Tomas is not a doctor of psychiatry. He does not have the credentials to determine the sanity of the accused."

"I will rephrase the question."

There was silence while Cloverfield moved across the floor. Back and forth. A minute passed, and then another. The tension was building, but he was just being theatrical. "In your opinion, Mr. Tomas, why do you think the accused didn't hear the screams for him to stop?"

"Like I said earlier, it was like he was out of his mind."

"No more questions."

Purcell stood and shuffled across the floor. "Permission to re-examine."

McBean cracked the knuckles of his fingers and stretched. "For what purpose?"

"Clarity."

The more he had to do with the little lawyer the more he admired him. "Will this take long?"

"Not at all." He held up his thumb and forefinger of his right hand and spoke. "I'll be brief."

"Permission granted."

Thank you, Your Honor. "Mr. Tomas, have you ever studied medicine?"

"Can't say that I have."

"Are you a doctor?"

"Nope."

"Have you ever studied psychiatry?"

"I don't even know what that means?"

The public gallery chuckled, and even the judge smirked.

Purcell's voice was warm and educational. "It is the study of the human mind, in order to understand how and why we think and operate the way we do."

"No."

"Thank you. That is all."

McBean waited for Tomas to find a seat. "How many more witnesses does the prosecution intend to call?"

"Two, Your Honor."

He turned his attention to the defense. "How many witnesses does the defense wish to call?"

"Two, Your Honor."

"Very well, we will continue in one hour. Court is adjourned."

The bailiff's voice was unnecessarily loud. "All rise."

The court was cleared, and a heavy silence settled over the room.

CHAPTER 31

Dwight Fotheringham strode into court like a man on a mission. He was tall and long of limb. His face was set in a permanent scowl, altogether he looked discontent with the world and his place in it. In truth, he was a blacksmith and preferred his own company. He found people useful when he needed to, and he spent the rest of his time avoiding civilization.

Millie Tippet waved coyly at the accused, who responded in kind. She was lost in a world of her creation. There was no doubt she felt connected to the man. Shared experiences or delusion of mind being the cause. She was planning to visit him, unexpectedly of course, that evening at the jailhouse. She didn't know what she'd say, nonetheless she was excited and nervous for the occasion. She wondered what he sounded like. Was his voice deep, harrowing, and troubled or was it waspish and childish. Either way she wasn't concerned. All she knew is that she had to hear him speak. To be close to him. To offer him some guidance and solace in his time of need. Afterall, it was just as the sheriff had said, the Christian thing to do.

Merle Overall had fallen asleep. Unfortunately, the ravages of time had caught up with her. It happened overnight, as it does with most people. She snored gently; Walter stood by the door. He looked at her and felt a pang of regret. He had always fancied her, and he suspected that Merle was secretly smitten with him. They had grown old apart and the life that they could have had together eluded them both.

Thomas Bland sat with his meaty and thick forearms across his large stomach. His face was in a permanent scowl. Thick lips and protruding eyebrows coursed his dark and moody eyes. He was a man to watch. His wife, Marjorie, was never seen in public. An agoraphobic, she spent her time knitting and reading by a dim light, in a cold room. She hadn't always been that way. In her youth Marjorie graced the day with a smile and a skip in her step. She spoke lightly and earnestly. Once so demure, yet now so withdrawn. There's no telling of the influence of one person on another. Some can shrug off the influence, while it absorbs others. Bland watched the proceedings with muted interest. He was there because others were there, and no one wanted to miss out.

Mavis Williams sat on the edge of the bench. She was a little uncomfortable, but she wouldn't miss it for the world. Each night she would sit at her favorite chair, at the table her mother had imported from New York, and write. She would, to her account, recall the proceedings and write them down as she either remembered them or wanted others to remember them. Isn't that history though? she asked herself when she began to have pangs of guilt for bending the truth a little. She would sit up until midnight and beyond scribbling away. It gave her life some meaning.

Miles Hammond' color was off. He looked peaked, and a little sick. Still, he wrote in his pad, yet not with the fervor of previous efforts. His demeanor was noticed and commented on by all significant inquirers as to the cause of his malaise.

"No further questions, Your Honor."

"Thank you, Mr. Purcell. Mr. Cloverfield, you may cross-examine."

It was unseasonably hot inside the courtroom, and the big man was sweating. He removed his light blue jacket, which was coated in sweat. The sweat stains of his shirt, under the armpits reflected the warmth in the room. Either that or he was hyper nervous. Every move he made had been heavily scrutinized and inflated to the point of buffoonery. He was made the scapegoat of the trial thus far. He was also contemplating suing Hammond for slander regardless of whether he printed another bad word about him or not. He was convinced that any judge would find in his favor. He was a lawyer and knew the law.

"Thank you. Mr. Fotheringham, why did you try to stop the fight?"

"The accused had lost control."

"How did you try to stop the fight?

"I yelled at him to stop."

"How many times did you yell at him to stop?"

"Definitely once, perhaps twice, but no more than that."

"In your opinion did he hear you?"

"No."

"Why not?"

"It was like he was somewhere else."

"Could you please explain what you mean by that to the court?"

"He didn't hear me, besides he just seemed intent on hurting poor Mr. Jenkins."

"You just said that he seemed intent, but is it possible as you described less than two minutes ago that he had indeed lost his mind?"

"Yes, either one is probable."

He changed tone and tact. "How tall are you Mr. Fotheringham?"

"Six-foot, three inches tall."

"How much do you weigh, sir."

"Two-hundred and twenty pounds."

Cloverfield turned his attention to McBean. "Your Honor, I know that Mr. Fotheringham has stated his profession to the court, however, in context on this line of questioning may I ask him to state it again."

"Very well, you may."

He bowed slightly and nodded to the bench as a sign of respect. "Mr. Fotheringham, could you please reiterate your profession to the court."

"Blacksmith."

"When the esteemed Mr. Purcell questioned you, you stated that you tried to physically remove the accused from the deceased. Is that correct?"

"That's correct."

"Were you able to remove the accused?"

"No."

"Do you consider yourself strong?"

"Yes, I need to be in my profession."

"How did the accused respond to you trying to remove him?"

"He shrugged me off?"

"Did you try again?"

"I was planning to step in and wrap my arms around his neck, but Sheriff Wells came along and defused the situation."

"How did he defuse the situation?"

"He struck the accused across the back of the head with the barrel of the shotgun and knocked him out."

"Thank you, Mr. Fotheringham. Your Honor, the defense has no more questions."

"Court is adjourned until ten am tomorrow morning," barked McBean.

CHAPTER 32

Walter escorted Merle Overall to her small abode. He held her by the crook of the elbow and guided her slowly through the deserted streets. Most citizens were filling the bars and cafes of main street. It was the regular thing to do at the end of the day's proceedings. The sun was high and biting. The heat was relentless, and Merle felt every sting of the rays on her face.

"You don't have to walk me home Walter. I can manage."

"Tsk, tsk. Now Merle, you could barely keep your eyes open in court. It's my duty and honor to escort you home and I'll have no more complaints from you."

Merle knew that she couldn't have made it by herself, and she made no more fuss, but they both knew that she was eternally grateful for the comfort. There was a welcome silence. Their bodies close together and a feeling that only fondness for another can generate swept through them. They enjoyed the moment.

The gate was squeaky, and Walter made a note to oil the hinges the first chance he got. Merle fumbled in her purse for the key and opened the door. He helped her inside, and she sat at the kitchen table. A little shaky and faint; she sat heavily in the chair.

"Don't you move."

Merle didn't respond. She closed her eyes and breathed deeply. Walter went next door to where the Gilberts resided. They were an older couple and had given up on the outside world years earlier. The only time they were spotted around town was when they were required to purchase goods for their day-to-day necessities. His knock startled them and when Agnus peeked through the curtain and saw the stressed look of Walter, she knew something was wrong.

The door opened hastily. "Walter. What's wrong?" He hitched a thumb to his left. "It's Merle, she's not well. Can you watch her while I fetch the doc?"
Without a word she scurried down the steps and went to her neighbor's assistance.

Walter walked as fast as he could to find Doctor Irving Von Klaus. He was a temperamental old cuss, yet as sharp as a Sunday confession. Klaus emigrated from Germany twenty years earlier. He was carried across the sea in a ship called the Brummer. He left behind unfavorable conditions, an ungrateful family, and an impending lawsuit for malpractice.

The door opened violently, and he was violently pulled from the journal he was reading, called '*Treatise on the Oath of Natural Remedies*' by Flora Leur.

Walters' voice fell out of him like rapids over a waterfall. "Doc, you've got to come quick. Merle has had a turn for the worse."

Without having time to absorb the intruder's words he grabbed his valise and locked the door on his way out. His accent was still strong. "What appears to be the matter?"

Walter explained as best he could. He walked two paces ahead of the doctor and in a few brisk minutes he led him through the door of Merle's home where they met Agnus in the kitchen. She had a genuine look of concern on her face.

"I have just put her to bed. She looks so awfully pale. Through this way, Doctor Von Klaus."

"Thank you." He turned and held Walter at bay. "You stay here now. You'll be no use to me in there."

Agnus led the doctor down the hallway to Merle's room. She said over her shoulder as she left. "I have water on the boil and the coffee is hot."

Walter moved to the front door and closed it before returning to pour himself a coffee. He had let opportunity slip between his fingers. For fear of rejection, he had refused to act on his feelings. The consequence was loneliness. And this he confessed as he prayed for Merle. He also promised to redeem himself if given the chance. He prayed for this as well.

CHAPTER 33

Millie Tippet entered the sheriff's office with her purse in front of her, and her evening hat pinned tightly to golden hair. Her fragile frame was silhouetted against the window by the fading light. She appeared weak of body yet determined of mind. "Good evening, Sheriff Wells."

"Good evening, Miss. Tippet. He stood and moved the chair from his desk across to the cell. Opening the door the carpenter fixed in place, he sat the chair in front of the open cell door. "You have a visitor, Noble."

He was sitting on the edge of the bed reading the bible. He raised his head, assumed it was his lawyer and moved across to the door.

"You have forty minutes."

Wells moved across to the window, as the visitor stepped lightly to the cell. Her voice was a whisper, though she never intended it to be so. "Hi. My name is Millie, Millie Tippet."

Noble was stunned but delighted to see her. He knelt on the ground before the cell bars and grabbed them.

Smiling, he displayed his crooked teeth. His voice was weak yet desperate. It was as if he hadn't spoken for a month. His lawyer has not visited him in the cell for some time and spoke briefly to him each morning. He was starved for conversation. "I guess you know who I am."

She nodded. "How are you feeling?"

His lips were moist, as were his eyes. He was on the verge of tears. "Lonely and scared."

She reached her hand toward him, and he grasped her hand gently. It was feminine and pale. Delicate and sensual. He smelled her skin and sighed. Millie loved the attention. She had never had the attention of a man before and the thought pleased her.

"I've seen you every day at the trial," he whispered.

"And" she said determinedly, "I will be there every day for as long as the trial takes." She admired his hands, and failed to understand how they could have caused Mr. Jenkins, who she considered a ruffian and a fool, death.

He stared at her, not knowing what to say. He considered her a finer class of lady than Delores the whore. It was Noble's way though. Like others, he clung to the first person that paid him attention. Millie was no different. She put faith in the architect of her understanding of Noble, Miles Hammond. She admired the editor for his use of words and his ability to touch her heart with such eloquent turns of phrase.

She sighed, bowed her head, and fiddled with the purse in her lap. "Have you been reading the Bible, and praying?"

"All day and every night. That's all I do."

Her eyes were crystal blue. He stared longingly into them and sensed a love he had never felt before. Her voice was as soft as silk, yet her words carried the weight of an anvil. "Deuteronomy 31:6."

He twisted his head to the side. He couldn't remember the chapter or the verse, nor could he pick up on the message she was sending him. "I'm sorry, my memory is failing me."

She smiled. A straight row of teeth, not like Dolores. Her teeth were crooked and brown. They also smelled of smoke. Millie's breath was sweet, like peppermint. "*Be strong and of a good courage, fear not, nor be afraid of them: for the LORD thy God, he it is that doth go with thee; he will not fail thee, nor forsake thee."*

"I hope you're right. Though my faith will be tested, I'll continue to pray for freedom."

She scrunched her face up. "You will only find freedom through forgiveness."

They sat in silence. Noble was ruing the day he rode into Rocksprings. He rewound the clock and imagined a life with Millie Tippet. It was a wonderful life. A white picket fence. Two children. A boy and a girl. Church on Sundays. Evenings by the fire. But that's all they'd ever be, ideals. Yet ideals had a way of shaping our insecurities into strengths. Of blending the past with the future, at the expense of both. Of deluding us into thinking that things would ever be okay when we knew in our heart of hearts that they wouldn't. Of running away from our dilemmas instead of confronting them head on. Of seeking freedom from want. Possessing the need to desire. Controlled by a jealous urge, the surge of emotions swept through him. It was a feeling of regret and of anger. Of disappointment and sadness. He stood, cussed, and moved across to the bunk. She stood and grabbed hold of the cell bars.

"Timothy."

He cried. He put his face in the palm of his hands and cried. It turned into a sob. He fell to the knees and wept. His back to her.

"Timothy." Her voice was pleading.

Sheriff Wells heard everything, and he moved stealthily across to the cell. "Visiting time is up."

Miss. Tippet gathered the pleats of her dress in her hands, scurried across the floor and made her way hastily through the door.

CHAPTER 34

Night fell over Rocksprings as it had since the beginning of time. The sun struggled to maintain its grip on the land but gave way to nature's will. Night may have fallen upon the town, but darkness made its way through the streets, alleys and roads that led to and through the once reserved, sheltered and quiet settlement. Dark thoughts and plans were considered. Lust, greed and desire, cruel desire crippled one man's mind. His thoughts were twisted. His intent fired by an instinctual urge. Like a ravenous wolf that stalks its prey. He waited for the silence to become heavy. Most of the decent citizens retired early. They rose with the sun to start the day. They plied their trades and passed their time in honest labor. They toiled seeking favor from nothing except their time spent in honest interactions with the earth and one another. It was a simple life. Though routine was monotonous on occasion, it was a pious life. Without piety, and community, what is there to hang your hat on at night? The same inherent qualities that make us feel like we belong, and connected are the same pursuits we consume ourselves with. One gives birth to another, and thus an equilibrium is maintained. But not all people think alike. There are those that take what others have earned or created. They seek to benefit from the toil of others. Their thoughts don't see the world as decent folk. Their world is greyer. Rain falls on the horizon. A strong wind sweeps dirt in their face. Antagonized and on edge. They wedge themselves between the moral and immoral and walk both sides of the fence. They pilfer and scratch for crumbs like rats. They feed on the carcass of society like vultures. They destroy what others have created. They steal what others have earned. There is a lesson to be learned yet their minds are warped. Their thinking is skewed. The selfish live side by side with the noble. Dishonesty erodes truth. Adultery defies purity. The lure of the curse is strong, but there is a right and wrong. It's as crisp and as clear as a winter's frost. The cost of life is the price of death. Bereft and afraid they lay in the shadows. Crawling across the surface of society, infecting life with decay. Laying the seeds of doubt, anguish, and sorrow. Consumed only with tomorrow. Short-sighted and unsatisfied. Compelled to act. Driven by a desire. An addict, a fool, a dolt. It's your fault. On the edge, unaccepted, rejected, buried beneath an inept and uncaring world. There is darkness in light as there is light in despair. Why should the disengaged care? Murderous intent doth lurk close by.

He waited patiently. His mouth was dry. He removed the flask from his hip pocket and took an unholy swig. Wiping his lips with the back of his hand he heard voices from within. He moved deeper into the darkness that secreted his form. This was the second night in a row he had waited. Waiting for an opportunity. The right time to strike. Alas, it wasn't to be. Not tonight. He recoiled and retraced his steps. He scurried across the northern end of main street. Heading west. He paused. A dog barked twice. A light came on in a window to his left. Back to the wall. Cautiously, and with a thrill that brought him alive, he moved. Pausing before the window. Staring through the curtain he saw a chair by the bed nestled in the corner of the room. A bible on the bedside table. Noises from beyond. Footsteps on the hardwood floor. A man entered and closed the door. It was an old man he didn't recognize. He looked well past his age. Crippled and bent. A lonely life, and a searching death. He crawled into bed, picked up the bible and read. Moving past the moment, he turned right, and left. Pausing at a door he removed a key and slid it expertly into the lock and without a sound unlocked the door and stepped inside. Breathing easier, and self-satisfied he found his way to his kitchen. It was there he opened the drawer, and removed the long blade from deep with his coat pocket and added it to the drawer's contents.

It was time to rest. He moved beyond the room on his left. It belonged to his wife, and she rarely came out, at least while he was home. And though he tried to let sleep consume him his mind was riddled with thoughts. He would have to strike, and soon. He couldn't sustain the pressure any longer. Joe Denning had extended the draft one too many times. When he pleaded with him for one more extension, Denning was adamant it would be the last. That day was approaching. He needed money to service his debts, or he would lose everything he had. He could lose his wife though she meant less to him than his business and his home.

His predicament was that he owed the bank money. Lots of it. The debts brought about his lust for gambling. He was addicted. Most nights he would be at the Western Palace risking it all for the chance of a little more. The owners of the Palace, Francis, and Dior Favell were like vultures. They picked the carcass of the patrons clean. They would be seen sitting at a small table at the end of the balcony on the second floor of the Palace and watching proceedings below. They were night owls. They waded through the night and slept through the day. Mince, their trusted servant. In a room upstairs, in their private room was a safe. It was rumored to contain as much money as the bank and it was this, he at first considered robbing for his personal benefit. He considered it his money. There were a few problems with this plan when he thought about it in the light of day. The first being that he didn't know the combination, and thus he would have to force someone to divulge the combination, and then he would have to kill them. This could get messy considering the location of the safe and the number of whores who called the Palace home.

His next target was Denning, the banker. But this idea was soon dispensed with. Despite his predicament he had a fondness for the banker. Besides, he had seen the bank's vault, it was no doubt more difficult to crack and or to dispense with. He would also have to find the accounts and records and destroy them all. This was too complicated a task. He liked simple things. He couldn't contemplate more than one or two things at a time. That's why he shouldn't have gone into business. He simply didn't have a head for figures. He couldn't plan and had no fiscal integrity.

He picked his new target. It was Miles Hammond. Hammond had been selling a lot of papers lately and by his estimation would have enough money to alleviate some of his stress, which is if he didn't gamble it away. The problem was that Hammond was rarely alone at night when the murder must take place. That old coot, Wiley Johns, spent every minute with him, but he had to find a way. He simply had to act.

The other choice he had was to steal from people's homes, but he doubted they had much. This would require many break ins, and each one making it more difficult for the next to be carried out successfully. The residents would soon fortify their abodes and were apt to shoot at anything that moved and be justified in doing so by the law. This proposition was too risky. Whatever choice he made, he would need to strike for time was short and eternity long.

On the next night that graced Rocksprings, tragedy would strike.

CHAPTER 35

"The prosecution calls Sheriff Otis Wells to the stand."

A general sigh passed through the court room as Wells walked purposely to the stand, muttered the oath, and sat heavily. The chair squeaked under the weight of his rough treatment.

Purcell was feeling spry. He looked dapper, as he always did in a pinstripe suit with a dark blue tie. He bounced to his feet and scurried across the floor.

"Please state your name and occupation for the court."

"My name is Otis Wells, and I am the Sheriff of Rocksprings."

"How long have you been sheriff?"

"About four years."

"I have a couple of questions about the night Mr. Jenkins was murdered."

Cloverfield's voice was crisp and sharp. "Objection Your Honor. The accused remains the accused until determined otherwise by the court. Need I remind the esteemed Mr. Purcell that he is to refrain from referring to the defendant as a murderer?"

The prosecutor snapped his heels together and bowed toward the bench. "Your Honor, I will rephrase the statement."

McBean had presided over many murder trials. There was a time that a woman poisoned her husband slowly over a year by lacing his dinner with rat poison. Turns out that he couldn't taste the poison because he was always drunk and violent. Another time a man murdered his business partner over a deal gone wrong. He recalled the case where John Oliver murdered his wife so he could leave her for his mistress. Oliver was slow in responding to his lover's demands and she moved on. Such cases instilled in him a sense of vigor and honor. It was a time in his life when he believed that he was making a difference. He was young, strong, and full of acid and vinegar. He didn't take a backward step. He delighted the upper echelons of polite society. He was a storyteller, with diction and tone that matched every turn of phrase. He was always professional, but this case was tiring. It had been running less than a week with only a few more days to go before the jury would retire for a verdict, and he wanted to step down. This trial would be his curtain call. He had saved enough money over the years, and he would head east or west to the coast and enjoy the summer breezes and the cool ocean water.

As a lawyer he argued in some of the most high-profile courtrooms of the country. His record was impressive with only one sour moment which he preferred not to dwell on. He was a tyrant in the courtroom, and possessed a restless energy that couldn't be matched. However, a series of instances in which he witnessed the wheels of justice manipulated for political and economic gain turned him against the profession he once admired. The legal system was self -perpetuating. It was barbaric. A man had to fight to earn his reputation and even harder to keep it. It had nothing to do with justice, and everything to do with winning. It was how the system was structured. Opponent against opponent. Who had the best argument won the case. Forget equality and fairness. They were lazy ideals invented by lazy people. He almost drifted off in thought before responding to the current objection before him.

"Very well, continue."

"Sheriff, I have just a few questions for you about the night Mr. Jenkins was killed, and then you may be dismissed."

Wells nodded. He had given evidence before, but it was usually in cases of assault, nothing as serious as this. There had been a murder before he took office, but he didn't recollect much of the detail. A man was accused of murdering his wife but took his own life not long after. The previous lawman buried the case. It was his brother-in-law. Sometimes when we think we are doing the right things we're just not.

Wells nodded.

"The court has heard earlier testimony that Mr. Fotheringham tried to remove the accused from the deceased lifeless body but was unable to do so. Did you witness this?"

"Yes."

"How?"

"With my eyes?"

The courtroom broke into a fit of laughter. It was funny because the sheriff was anything but funny. In fact, he had no sense of humor at all. That's what made the statement hilarious. He was still feeling a little off from the day before. He didn't sleep and the whole situation was stressing him out. He was fed up and wanted life to resume to normal. He had no doubt that given time life would resume as normal, without the hoopla that now consumed the town.

When the laughter subdued after a few claps of McBean's wearisome gavel, Purcell continued. "Quite humorous, Sheriff. Please describe in detail what you remember from the night in question."

"It was a typical Friday night I believe. The usual revelers were out enjoying the end of the working week. I had just finished making the rounds and was writing a report when I heard the commotion. It happened so fast. By the time I worked out what was happening the crowd had swelled considerably. I heard someone shouting and screaming, and as I broke my way through the crowd, I witnessed Mr. Fotheringham try to pull the accused off the deceased. He failed, and as he stepped forward to try again, I stepped between them and laced the accused with the barrel of the Greener."

"For the purpose of the court, could you please clarify what a Greener is?"

"A shotgun."

"What happened then?"

"I dispersed the crowd and sent for the doctor. I checked the vital signs of the deceased, but there were none. Then I dragged the accused to the jailhouse and locked him up. I went back to the deceased. By this time, he was lying in the dust covered in blood. Von Klaus was there, and he merely shook his head indicating that the man was dead. I sent for the undertaker and followed the procedure in such circumstances."

"When was the accused charged with murder?"

"The following afternoon after I had collected witness statements."

"Thank you, Sheriff. No more questions."

"You may cross-examine, Mr. Cloverfield."

He was in fine form this morning. He was secretly worried that his star witness, doctor of psychiatry, Owen Restful, would be late to testify, but before court he received a message from Walter that Restful would be arriving on the afternoon stage out of Telegraph.

"Sheriff, do you always assault those you arrest."

"Objection." Purcell continued. "Your Honor, this line of questioning is unconstitutional. Not for the first, second or third time have I had to object to such barbarous questioning. This man," pointing to the lawman, "is an esteemed pillar of this community. His reputation is not on trial."

"Sustained. Your line of questioning is immature, Mr. Cloverfield. You will rephrase your question. If you continue to use that language in MY court, you will be found in contempt. This is your final warning. Do you understand me?"

"Yes." Cloverfield's voice was too soft for the judges liking and when he asked the question, he did so sharply that all people in the courtroom jumped.

"Do you understand me?"

Cletus was done. He had run out of steam. Though he had convinced Timothy Noble that he could win the case he had failed to convince himself. He dressed slovenly and was awkward in his movements. His speech was discourteous and unprofessional. Still, there are many types that make the legal system tick over. Good and bad.

For better and for worse. The wheels of '*justice*' stopped for no one.

"Yes, sir,"

"Continue."

"Why did you feel the need to whack the accused with the Greener?"

"Efficiency."

A wry chuckle ran through the public gallery.

"Can you explain that statement?"

"Well, I figure that a man who is punching a lifeless body is not in the mood for discussion. At that time, I didn't know the state of Jenkins. All I knew is that I had to bring an end to the assault, and that seemed the most efficient manner in doing so."

"I see," Cloverfield mused, "in your opinion was the man out of his mind?"

"Can you clarify what you mean by, out of his mind?"

CC wasn't anticipating the question and he stumbled over his words. "Well, you know, out of his mind?"

"If I knew I would not have asked you to clarify."

More laughter.

"Was he out of control?"

"Out of control, yes, but isn't that different from being out of your mind?"

Once more the lawyer was caught off guard. He tried to make light of it. "I thought I was the lawyer." It was a lame attempt at a joke, and no one laughed. The public gallery had already decided that they didn't like him. Some of them had decided this well before the death of Jenkins. Their interactions with the man had been a negative experience. He was loud and obnoxious. Overconfident and overbearing.

"Could you please just answer the question?"

"I couldn't say with confidence either way?"

Wells made notice that the dynamics of the public gallery changed. Merle was absent, as was Walter. Hammond was scribbling as usual, and Bland sat with his arms folded across his chest staring into space. Doris was noticeably absent, and Mavis Williams was sitting in Merle's spot by the door. Hammond' article was quite mundane. It was just a rundown of the court proceedings of the day before. There was no outlandish headline, and Cloverfield was not mentioned in the article at all.

"Couldn't or won't."

Wells shrugged. The lawyer was doing his job. No hard feelings. "Couldn't."

The defense counsel had nothing. "That'll be all Your Honor."

"Thank you." Before McBean could speak another word Purcell interjected.

"Your Honor, I have one question and one question only for the Sheriff. May I?"

"Make sure it is one question."

The little man nodded. "How many times did you hit the accused with the barrel of the shotgun?"

"Once."

"Thank You, the prosecution rests its case."

McBean's gravelly and tired voice echoed off the walls. "Adjourned until ten am tomorrow morning."

CHAPTER 36

People filed out of the courthouse. It was a little before noon and the sun scorched the earth. A lonely rider heading into town from the east trailed a flat eared mule. The onlookers shielded their eyes from the sun and watched the rider carefully. Those with eyes capable of doing so noticed the rider and the load of the mule. A strange voice remarked. "It's Festus Rasmussen and there's a body over that mule."

A smattering of voices found their way along the front of the courthouse and through the door until they reached a crescendo. There were some terse murmurings and people began stepping aside for Wells. He glanced over his shoulder and barked an order at Swan. "Get him," he pointed to Noble, "into the back room and don't come out until Wilson or I say otherwise."

"Make way for the sheriff."

People stood aside and as he stepped into the sunlight. He squinted against the bright light, rubbed his stomach, and said to himself, "blasted indigestion."

Moving to the end of the porch he saw Festus, bloody from fingertip to elbow and all over his face. Wrapped in Hessian, thrown across the back of a lank, lean, and nasty looking mule was a human carcass. Wells stepped into the street. Walked to the middle where Festus reined his horse.

He patted the neck of the bay that carried the big man's weight. "Easy boy, easy does it." He searched the big man's face, and watched as a tear breached the point of no return and ran down his face. Festus, what's going on here."

More tears streamed down his ruddy complexion leaving their mark on his bloody face. "It's Deadeye, Sheriff. He done gone and blown his face off."

Wells looked at the body with apprehension and trepidation. It was an all-consuming moment. Gripped by fear he moved across to the moody mare who was showing signs of restlessness. He tried to sooth it as he pulled the hessian aside and saw the remnants of Deadeye. His face was chewed to pieces. He gulped heavily and tried to regain composure.

"How did this happen, Festus?"

Fighting back tears he managed, "cleaning that shotgun of his. He was always cleaning it. That gun was cleaner than a duck."

"Looks fresh. When did it happen?"

"This morning, a little after sunup."

"Okay, Festus. Head to my office and I'll send for the undertaker."

He nudged the bay and lumbered slowly down the street.

People followed from a distance wanting to know who was strapped to the mule. Likewise, Wells stepped quickly, but not before turning and asking a local man by the name of Mannah to fetch both the doctor and the undertaker.

Festus reigned up, dismounted, and hitched the bay. He dipped his head into the trough and scrubbed his face clean. Bland stepped forward and removed the hessian. "Deadeye. It's Deadeye."

Festus shooed him away like a fly. Bland smiled wryly and moved aside. By the time Festus climbed the steps and entered the office a few of the braver men had also looked at the dead man.

Rasmussen was breathing hard. Wells motioned him to sit, and he plunked himself down in the chair, and then went outside to hunt the onlookers away. They moved across to the shade to the other side of the street and watched the proceedings.

Festus spent the next hour telling and retelling the same story repeatedly. Wells asked probing questions, but his story didn't change. Deadeye was cleaning the gun when it discharged at close range. Of course, the Sheriff doubted such a thing, but experienced people had accidents doing the routine activity they had performed for years. His nephew shot his own foot off, despite being adept at gunplay and safety conscious. Accidents happen all the time, they just don't always happen to the people we know. Like Doris, Festus was illiterate and made his mark once the lawman wrote and read the statement to him.

Von Klaus and the undertaker arrived but were duly given their instructions and moved on to carry out their orders. It was midafternoon and Rasmussen had a thirst that needed quenching.

"Where will you be staying?"

The defeated man shrugged his shoulders. "Don't know. Don't care."

"Don't leave town. I may have further questions. "

Wells watched him leave, cross the street and head to the Western Palace. The onlookers followed in his wake. He considered the situation. A dead man and his friend. Festus brought his friend into town. When the lawman asked why he brought him into town instead of digging a grave at the mine. To this he didn't have an answer. He just shrugged his shoulders, cried, and said he didn't know. Still, a cold-blooded killer would not act like Festus had. He would hide the crime and flee. His actions were not suspicious. On the contrary his actions were anything but suspicious. He was musing on these thoughts when Von Klaus made a subdued entrance.

"What's the verdict, Doc?"

"Death by gunshot. Close range. Sometime this morning."

"Murder or accident?"

"There are burn marks and powder on his skin, or what's left of it. Hard to say. No way of knowing for sure, but the gun that killed him was fired at close range."

"Thanks, Doc." The doctor's report aligns with Rasmussen's recount of events.

Von Klaus nodded solemnly and left the lawman to his thoughts.

CHAPTER 37

The key turned in the lock and Swan yawned. "I'll be glad when the trial is over." He nudged Noble in the back, "come on man, get moving." He locked the cell door.

Poole laughed. "You get ornery when you're tired. A few more days, and you'll be sleeping like a baby."

They moved across to the fire and poured a mug of coffee. Poole was as exhausted as Swan, but their job wasn't done yet, so there was no use complaining.

Swan yawned again. "Do you think the jury will find Noble guilty?"

"Hard to say for sure. Ask me again when Cloverfield wraps this case up."

Swan nudged Poole and moved to the door. He opened it just in time for Millie Tippet to enter.

He smiled at her and closed the door behind her. "Leave your purse on the desk and move to the cell."

"It has my bible in it." She reached for her purse, "may I?"

"Sure."

She fussed for a moment and moved across to the chair Swan had placed in front of the cell door. "Forty minutes."

She felt that he was too abrupt and harsh. She sat down and tried her best to ignore him. He had a reputation with the ladies. She was not impressed.

Swan returned to Poole. "What do you think she is doing here?"

Poole held the enamel mug in both hands. "What do you mean?"

Swan was having a conversation with himself. Poole made it his business not to make other people's lives his business. Besides, his sister was pregnant and due any day now. He was making a list of names he didn't like.

Swan persisted. "I don't buy the whole Christian duty thing. There's not much to do in court except watch people, and I've noticed a few things."

He was expecting Poole to contribute to the conversation. Instead, Poole made a mental note of Ezekial and Sebastian. He didn't like those names.

When he didn't reply, Swan continued. "I've noticed the waves and the smiles. It's like they were flirting. They have a thing for one another. That must be it. It's the only thing that makes sense."

He moved across to the cell and leaned against the wall. He smiled as he looked at them. Noble lifted his gaze and stared dumbfounded. Offended at the lawman's intrusion. For the first time Swan saw anger well in the prisoner. His eyes changed color and his body language shifted. The deputy smiled. Cocky and self-assured, he moved across to Poole. "She has a thing for him all right. I should have said something earlier. What makes a semi-attractive woman attracted to a killer?"

Poole still wasn't paying attention. It wasn't on purpose, he just had things on his mind. He decided that he liked Madeleine and Elizabeth, but not Sage.

They passed the rest of the time in silence as Miss. Tippet flirted with the prisoner. With five minutes left Swan interrupted them and announced that visiting time was over. Both felt cheated out of time with one another, but neither of them made a noise of complaint. When the woman left, the lawmen hung their cups up and took care of some paperwork.

"Deputy." The prisoner called out.

"What do you want?"

"I want the young deputy, Swan."

Intrigued, they both moved across to the prisoner, but it was Swan who spoke. "What do you want?"

"You keep your hands and eyes off Miss. Tippet." Poole laughed. Swan was seething. "What are you saying, Noble?"

"She's a God-fearing woman and doesn't need the likes of you giving her a hard time."

"You're out of your mind." They both turned to walk away, but what the prisoner said next stopped them dead in their tracks.

"If you touch her, I'll kill you."

Poole went to the table and fussed for pencil and paper. Swan stared at Noble. There was plenty he wanted to say, but he did not say one word. Instead, he just smiled smugly while Poole wrote the date, time, and the statement down.

CHAPTER 38

Festus Rasmussen, the lone owner of the mines that he and his deceased partners Jake Jenkins and Deadeye Dave once shared, drowned his sorrows. He absorbed liquor like a plant absorbs light. The moment he stepped into the Western Palace a beer was pushed into his hand and a courteous hand slapped him on the back and escorted him to the bar. Men whooped and hollered. They felt his sorrow at losing a close friend. They mourned his loss and empathized with his woe. Most importantly they all found out what they wanted to know. Deadeye Dave, a loner, and a drifter after the war, was killed accidentally while cleaning his prized weapon.

"He was the most honest and loyal friend I ever had," moaned Rasmussen.

Doris pushed between the hoard of men to the bar and tried her best to woo the big guy into some entertainment. He grabbed hold of her meaty waist, moved across to a table and sat as he pulled her to his lap. He perked up a little when she kissed him on the cheek. The men laughed and cheered.

A stranger yelled, with heartiness and cheer. "If she doesn't take your mind off of Deadeye then nothing will."

They laughed again and the crowd dispersed. Festus found himself alone with Doris. She removed all the cheer and brought all the sorrow to the surface. He was a lug head, but an emotional one.

Her voice was sweet and caring. Festus was the sole owner of a played-out mine. He was a man of property. That made him a man with money. A man with money, in Doris' eyes, real or imagined, was a man to take seriously. She had no intention of becoming a miner's wife, but if he sold the mine and decided to move east then anything was possible. She was a dreamer, and a schemer. She had it all figured out. "How are you really feeling?"

The man was solemn and cast his eyes to his navel. His thick lips were moist with beer. A most unattractive site, but money, aspiration and deceit often go hand in hand. "I'm as good as can…" he turned to gaze at her most pathetically, "as can be expected."

"You unfortunate thing. Let me get you another drink."

Meanwhile, night had fallen. Life washed across Rocksprings like paint across a canvas. A reimagining of life in the small town was near an end. A few more days and the trial would be over. Noble would be found guilty and either hanged or sent to prison for life. There was a divide amongst the increasingly unruly patrons of the Palace as to the just punishment. A scuffle broke out over this very thing, but after the instigator got a busted lip for his trouble, he forgot what the fight was over, and everyone rejoined the festivities.

Francis and Dior Favell sat at their table and watched the night unfold before them. Their servant, Mince, moved swiftly tending to their demands and the demands of the customers. His bald head was sweating profusely. The Favell's were from the long line of Favell's from Forde County east of Washington. They boasted royal lineage, but to the casual critic such claims are meaningless unless proof can be tended to account for such happenings. Still, there were those who tended to believe the lie. Just what royal blood was doing running a gambling and whore house in an out of the way town no one seemed to ask.

Francis was a dapper gentleman. Small in stature yet with a fiery temper. He smelled of a combination of whiskey and cologne. It was an exotic blend. He considered himself a benefactor to the half a dozen whores that called the Palace home. He was an egotistical cuss and apt to lash as sharply with his tongue as he did with his cane. Dior was demure and quaint. Subject to violent outbursts at staff, especially whores. "You have to whip them into shape," was one of her favorite sayings. She was awkward at polite and casual conversation. They complimented one another and seemed content in each other's company. They came into town on the stage seven years earlier with a valise full of money and a desire to get more.

Speaking of stages, Cletus Cloverfield met the afternoon stage. Thankfully, most of the citizens were enamored with the events that had unfolded in Rocksprings to take notice.

CHAPTER 39

Cloverfield looked at the man who sat across from him. He was a small man, disheveled and dressed in a worn corduroy jacket with mismatching pants. His eyes were withdrawn and opaque. Misty and intoxicated. His lips were full, and dry. His bottom lip bled from excessive peeling skin. His hands were filthy as was his once white shirt that was done up crooked, and the hems of which hung out over a rope which he used as a belt. His voice was croaky and pleading. "I need a drink. Just one drink."

He held his hand out. It shook. His fingers were long and slender. They belied his small stature. He looked pitiful. A poor excuse of a man. Just like his father. A Doctor of Medicine, and a self-confessed philosopher of life. More like a fool. Still, his son seemed well adjusted and made it to adulthood without fuss. He followed his father into the health profession, but instead of medicine he chose psychiatry. 'Fools medicine.' His father called it, though, 'quack science' was his favorite descriptor for his son's chosen profession.

At first, it was a successful profession choice. He married into money and fell out of love quickly and turned to drink to make living with her bearable. She divorced him. Her father, through his political and official connections, destroyed his reputation and his business. Drinking to relieve stress quickly turned to drinking to relieve the tedium of his life. It would be the death of him. No doubt about that. When Cloverfield met him a mere nine years earlier he was as sober as the sun. Life can cause wear and tear on some quicker than others.

The lawyer shook his head and leaned back in his chair. "No drink, Owen."

Owen Restful had never had a successful practice. Psychiatry, at least in this part of the country, was still in its infancy and while some people came around to the idea, most discarded it as no better than voodoo. Some even considered it an intellectual excuse for misbehavior. A justification for the ills of normality, as if such a thing as common morality existed at all. The man could bore a crowd for hours with his knowledge on the topic. There wasn't enough demand for his services. His father-in-law,

H. Harold Hardwick, upon divorce, gave Restful enough money to satisfy his meager desires, however, made him sign a contract to hold his tongue about his affairs of the heart. Hardwick was an obnoxious man with eyes of coal and a mouth that ran like an unwashed tap. Owen was wise enough to uphold his end of the bargain, except the few times he penned his feelings to his ex-wife in the form of immature and drunken poetry. She kept the poems of course and uses them to entertain her friends at tea parties.

He was desperate, "just one more drink. All I need is one."

Cloverfield walked to the window. Restful was to be his expert witness. He had the script written, all he had to do was remember it, but the man was a mess. There was no way he would be fine by the morning. As he was contemplating the dilemma, he watched the lights of the town extinguish. He lived too far away from the Palace to hear the revelry. He turned to look at the pathetic wimp, Restful. The case was in ruins. It had been a shambles from the start. Nothing was going his way. Hammond was antagonizing him, the people scoffed at him, and no doubt laughed when they read the articles. His demeanor in court was slovenly, and McBean was the usual unruly cuss he had always been. Purcell was too polite, just too kind to be trusted. He hated them all. He hated the legal fraternity. He cussed Noble, most of all he cussed himself. He had failed to find the spark he thought he had. In his estimation he was a good lawyer, down on his luck. That was it, when he finished this case he would head east, open a practice, and try again. That would be either the fourth or fifth career restart. Each one ending in disgrace of some sort. The first involved a woman. The second was a bad investment. He stopped. He couldn't relive the dilemma over again. Yet here he was, on the eve of the end of the trial and his expert witness was rotten drunk. Restful fell out of the stage when he opened the door. Dirt covered his gray jacket and brown pants. It was then he noticed that Restful was wearing his shoes on the wrong feet. Cloverfield heard a noise and turned back to the window just in time to see a figure scurry across the front of the building. The window shattered. Glass flew everywhere. CC dived to the floor, believing he was being shot at, he crawled behind his desk and cowered in safety. Restful stood and picked up the object that hit him in the back of the head. It was a rock and tied to a rock was a piece of paper.

"CC." His voice was suddenly more sober.

Sensing the immediate threat was over the lawyer stood. Shakily and with some apprehension he took the rock from the 'expert witness's' hands. He examined it closely. There was some blood on the paper. He moved around the table and examined Restful's head. There was a small cut. Immediately he began to formulate a plan. He removed the paper and unfolded it. A shiver ran down his back and fear consumed him when he read a single word, 'DED.'

CHAPTER 40

On the other side of the darkness, a man opens the drawer of his kitchen cupboard and removes a flat bladed knife. He holds it in his gloved hands high against the light of the moon that shone through the window, and smiles. The point was sharp and the edge smooth. He stowed the blade in his thick jacket, moved along the corridor and stopped before his wife's room. He reached out for the handle and turned the knob slowly. He opened the door and peered through the opening. The room was dark. He could hear her ragged breath. Through the gloom her outline beneath the blanket could be made out. She was a burden that needed to be disposed of. As soon as he cleared the current mess up, he would make her disappear. He had it all figured out. He would feed her lifeless carcass to the pigs. They would dispose of her in a night. There would be no trace.

He was feeling smug. Self-satisfied and confident. Closing the bedroom door, he walked down the hallway and entered the alley that ran behind his home. He glued his figure to the wall and moved slowly. He was oblivious to the events that had occurred earlier that night. It was now early morning. The streets were dark and quiet. He paused occasionally to make sure no one was around. After ten minutes he was able to peer into the offices of Miles Hammond. The main room was empty, but he could hear muted voices coming from the print room. He had to find a way to separate the men, Johns, and Hammond. Patience was not one of his virtues, though identifying what virtues he did possess was not easy. The man was a heathen and a slovenly dolt. People were his acquaintances out of fear more than any shared sense of loyalty. It was to be his night.

Luck favored the killer when ten minutes later the old pressman needed to take an urgent call of nature. The back door of the office opened, and Johns staggered through in a hurry, and stepped in great strides up the small rise to the outhouse. He held a small lantern in his hand as he fumbled with the door and latched it behind him. The man moved swiftly up the rise to an old fence that separated the property from the rundown old livery. It was here he stumbled across an old fence paling. He picked it up and weighed it in his hands. He smiled to himself. It would do, the man was old, and it wouldn't take long to dispatch him. Moving across to the outhouse he waited while the man finished his business and stepped into the night. The lantern guiding his way.

Johns closed the door behind him and sighed. The paling came sailing through the air and crashed into the back of his skull. He was a tough old buzzard, but he staggered and fell to his knees. The lantern fell to the ground and was snuffed out. He turned and looked over his left shoulder at his attacker. He identified him immediately. "Why?" That was all he managed to say before the paling came sailing through the air and landed flush on the top of his head. A third and fourth blow were followed by a fifth and sixth. The killer lost count. Each blow delivered with a contempt for humanity. When he finished, he dropped to his knees and checked Johns' pulse. None. He was dead. He considered it a job well done, stood and dragged the man's body back to the outhouse, threw the lantern down the business end and kicked dust over the blood.

He approached the back door of the office of the Rocksprings Rag and removed the knife from his jacket.

Stepping inside he moved cautiously. He peered into the pressroom and Hammond was busy working, with his back to the intruder. He lunged forward, but as he did his foot twisted on the creaky floorboards and Hammond, startled by the unusual noise, turned and they collided together against the machine and tumbled to the floor. They wrestled feverishly. The intruder had dropped the knife. Hammond forced a thumb into the man's eyes and ripped upward, laying a gash two inches long on the attacker's forehead. This incensed the killer, and he overpowered the newsman, rolled over on top of him and pinned him to the floor. Hammond stopped moving as his arms were held down by his attacker whose words came out of him in a rush. "Where's the money?"

"What money?" His voice was ragged, but his mind moved quickly. Hammond was trying to formulate a plan. He was trapped and his time was measured in seconds.

He spat the words, and drool, dribbled from his mouth. "The safe, where's the safe?"

"There's no money here." Hammond said the wrong thing. He responded truthfully to the question. He kept all his money in the bank.

Enraged, the man punched Hammond and broke his nose. A howl emanated from the reporter's throat which was quickly cut short as the big man wrapped his meaty hands around Hammond' throat. The reporter struggled from side to side, and he lashed out. His fingernails scratched flesh on the attacker's face and arms. Before too long his struggle waned as his strength failed him. He soon blacked out. His throat a bleak and black mess from the meaty pawprints.

Standing, the man searched for and quickly found the knife. Standing over the unconscious, yet still alive Hammond, he rolled him over on his stomach and cut his throat like he would a hog. A hasty search of the office found no money. He was as broke when he left the office as he was when he entered.

CHAPTER 41

He corked a bottle of whisky and took a hearty swig. Regret lay heavy on his thoughts, though this was laced with self-pity rather than out of any moral duty for those he had ripped from the land of the living. He was selfish. A cur. A mongrel that had no moral compunction. Where had his life gone wrong? It is hard to say. He woke up to the same day and went to bed on the same nights as the law-abiding and decent citizens of Rocksprings. It's just that he filled his time with different activities. He was impetuous and self-pitying. It was everyone else's fault. The world didn't bend his way. People didn't act as he demanded. They didn't bow down in front of him. It had always been that way. He could blame his father for being a brute, and a bastard, and he did. He blamed him for the lack of affection just as much as he blamed his mother for too much affection.

His parents always fought. From sun-up to sundown, they bickered. It was a hopeless union. They lived in a time where such nonsense was tolerated, if it went on in private no-one really cared. The same rules applied to everyone, and there was a lot of dysfunction and chicanery that went on behind closed doors. Yet there is more good than bad, for people are not solely the products of their upbringing. Who they become is also a consequence of the actions they take, the decisions they make and the willingness to accept the consequences of said actions. It was the same sentiment written by Old Man Dabrille in his letter to the editor of the Rocksprings Rag, a long time ago.

He took another swig and cussed. He had been a loudmouth all his life. He was critical of others and saw everyone else's faults but his own. He has bullied and harassed people his entire life. He has intimidated and antagonized others for his pleasure. He had acted irrationally, but spending a lifetime being a victim of your own actions can lead you to make brash and illogical decisions. That is exactly what he did. He sat at the kitchen table. Consumed by sorrow at his situation. The man didn't feel guilt. He wasn't built that way. Instead, he closed his eyes and sobbed. It was a pitiful sound from a loud and obnoxious man. If he ran, they'd suspect him of the murders. If he stayed, how would he explain the scratches on his arms and face? He would wear a long sleeve shirt. Part problem solved. He could explain the scratch on his face. His wife was out of her mind. Everyone knew it. She attacked him in one of her fits. It happened once before.

He held his hands to pray. "Lord Jesus Christ, thou died for my sins. Though great art thou, I ask for forgiveness. I offer thee my love, my dedication, and devotion. In return I ask that I find a way out of this mess. Amen."

He opened his eyes and for the first time noticed the blood on his hands and his clothes. He redressed and tore the bloody clothes into rags to stoke the morning fire. He worked by lantern light and made sure every drop of blood was removed. When he finished the golden lights of dawn filtered through the sky. Grabbing the bottle of whisky, he sat in his father's old chair in front of the fire. He sobbed and drank. He prepared lies and stories, excuses, and alibis. The more he drank the more his mind rolled in fear. He drank more until he eventually passed out in the chair. The empty bottle of whisky clattered to the floor.

CHAPTER 42

Cloverfield was animated and in an exuberant mood. He was at his most eloquent, and devastatingly brilliant when he lied, well, stretched the truth. He was doing that in the chambers of Judge McBean. Present were the usual suspects. Cloverfield marched back and forth across the floor. "The Honorable Owen Restful, at this very moment," he was quite animated, "is lying in bed, an innocent victim of a targeted attack on yours truly." He thumped his chest with open palms. "Doctor Von Klaus has indicated that there is every chance he is suffering from concussion." He removed a piece of paper from his shirt pocket. "I have a statement from Von Klaus that states in his professional opinion that the esteemed doctor of psychiatry, Owen Restful is incapable of testifying for two days."

Purcell was flabbergasted. "Two days is preposterous. This case must proceed."

McBean leaned back in his chair. "Are you suggesting that the court ignore professional medical advice and direct an expert witness to testify?"

"I would prefer it."

"Mr. Purcell, you didn't answer my question."

He shrugged his shoulders and was almost ready to give up. "I would like a second opinion."

"Excellent." McBean smiled. "Find me a doctor."

Purcell's usual stoic demeanor showed some signs of cracking. "We request that Mr. Restful is assessed again this afternoon, and again in the morning with the intention of resuming at ten o'clock tomorrow."

"Cloverfield, what is your response?" McBean sat back in his chair and folded his arms.

"Two days Your Honor."

"Mr. Purcell's request is reasonable. I will be present when Von Klaus inspects the witness."

The lawyers had something to say, but McBean didn't want to hear it. "This conversation is finished."

Inside the courtroom a restless public gallery waited impatiently. The accused waited in the dock. Swan stood next to him. He smiled and Noble tried to ignore him as he stared across the room to Millie Tippet, but privately he was seething.

Sheriff Wells stood by the bench and scoured the crowd. He had been watching the crowd for any signs. Signs of what, he wasn't quite sure of. He yawned. Cloverfield woke him no more than ten minutes after the incident with Restful. He had spent hours asking questions of the men involved, writing, and signing statements. It was becoming a taxing profession. Merle Overall was absent from her usual position. As was Walter. The citizens were creatures of habit and occupied the same places in the gallery, but something was off. Between Archie Howard and Faith Welling there was an empty space. Thomas Bland, the butcher, was missing. He was usually front and center being loud and intrusive. His absence was noted, as was that of Miles Hammond. One peculiarity was acceptable, but two at the same time made him feel funny. He moved across to the front door of the courthouse, opened it and called for Deputy Poole, who was rostered on to watch those coming and going.

Before he called out, he heard the bailiff call the court to order. He turned as McBean made his way through the door to the bench. Rocksprings was a small town, and everyone had heard and reheard the story involving Cloverfield, the rock and the expert witness.

The room fell silent. Waiting in anticipation. The air was electric. McBean was sympathetic, yet added to the intrigue by stating, "court dismissed till ten o'clock tomorrow morning."

Just as he finished speaking Walter barged through the courthouse door. The patrons of the room returned to the intruder. His face was ashen white. He was sweating. His voice was high and strained. "Sheriff, Sheriff, come quick, there's been a murder."

CHAPTER 43

Wells lifted the head of the deceased. Hammond was almost decapitated; such was the ferocity of the slash that severed his jugular vein. He would have been dead in minutes. He imagined life fading before his eyes as blood pumped onto the cold floor. The sickly ooze had congealed. In the heat the body deteriorated. The scene was macabre. The office had been ransacked. Blood covered the draws and the desk. Paper was strewn on the floor, and a chair lay on its side. The killer was searching for something. Such a beastly act had never occurred in the small town. He walked back and forth looking for signs of the killer. He paused before the dirty window and peered into the street. Wilson Poole and Thomas Swan were holding the crowd back. He saw condemning gazes and heard critical voices. The place they had come to call home had been spoiled by a vicious murder, and not so long ago a man was bashed to death in the main street. A killer was on the loose. The fear gripped them and rightly so. He wondered if the death was related to the case. Just like Cloverfield's incident with the rock.

Were they linked together? He had a lot to unravel, and for a man unexperienced in the complexities of figuring out the criminal mind he wasn't sure he was up to the task.

"Sheriff."

Wells turned and eyed Von Klaus and the undertaker. It was the medico who spoke. "Can we move the body now?"

He nodded and turned back to the window when he heard a scream emanating from the back yard. Wells pushed past the men and exited hastily through the back door. Sunlight tricked his eyes, and he sheltered them from the glare. Walter was standing at the top of the small rise. Looking like a ghost and unable to move he motioned the sheriff toward him. Without a word he pointed to the outhouse. Hesitantly the lawman opened the door and stared at the cold, battered, and bruised corpse of Wiley Johns.

"Doc. We have another one."

Thirty minutes later both bodies had been removed and the crowd dispersed. Wells was scribbling in the notepad. Swan kicked the dust and waited impatiently while Poole was sent back to the jail to watch the prisoner.

"Who would do such a thing, Sheriff?"

Without pausing he said, "hard to say for sure."

"Any idea why?"

"Looks like a robbery gone wrong."

"What will we do now?"

It was a simple question yet profound on so many levels. He simply had no idea. The murders obviously occurred late at night or early in the morning and he doubted there would be any witnesses. Hammond and Johns often worked late while the rest of the town slept. It was the nature of their profession. Nothing but a murder of opportunity. He reasoned that Hammond was the intended target and that Johns was merely dispensable. Money: logic informed him that the reason was motivated by greed.

"We'll ask around, but I doubt we'll find witnesses."

"What about Cloverfield and the rock?" Swan asked.

Wells put his pencil in his pocket and shrugged his shoulders. "No witnesses."

Swan moved restlessly and his hand fell to the butt of his revolver. He ran the fingertips over the smooth butt. "Seems strange don't you think that Festus rides into town and the lawyer is harassed, and the reporter is killed."

The sheriff yawned, "coincidental or not. He is the first person I intend to talk to."

CHAPTER 44

"Howdy, Mince."

The barman looked up from polishing the same spot on the bar. He had been thinking about Dior Favell. He was infatuated with the delicate woman. Her slender and weak demeanor attracted him. He wanted to be her protector and the only thing he decided that he could protect her from was the loveless clutches of her husband. Mince was loyal to the owners of the Palace only because of the lady of the house. He wanted to take her away from Rocksprings, but he didn't know where. He had never been more than half a dozen miles from the town in years. The world and its problems needed too much figuring out, and he didn't have a head for such thinking. Instead, he kept his desire to himself and pined for her in private. His look was distant, and he only half responded as enthusiastically as he should have.

His voice was lonely, and he tried to bring himself together but failed. "Hi, Sheriff."

Wells was perceptive enough to understand the sensibilities of moments such as these. "What's on your mind?"

"Just thinking is all. It's nothing. Not worth discussing."

Wells knew he was lying but let it slide. It's what most men did. "I'm looking for, Festus."

"Is that about what happened last night?"

The lawman ignored the probe. "Is he about?"

"Follow me, Sheriff." He tucked the Rag into his apron and led Wells up the stairs and along the hall. He walked slowly. A plod. He stopped on the third door on the left. Knocking three times he stepped back and wiped his hands down the leg of his pants. There was some noise from beyond the door, and a weary voice hastened along. "No need to knock so loud."

It was Doris, and when she opened the door, she looked atrocious. Her face was pale and showed severe signs of aging. She held a blanket wrapped around her and she appeared to stagger as if she was still intoxicated.

"What do you want?"

Wells was less decorous and polite as he was the last time they spoke. He pushed past her, and she stumbled to the side and fell against the door.

"Where is he?"

She yawned and rubbed her eyes. "Who?"

"Festus."

She fluffed and swayed behind the screen in the corner of the room. The blanket appeared over the edge and a brassiere disappeared, like a swimmer being dragged to the murky depths by a ravenous sea creature. Doris didn't say a word for two minutes while she dressed. When she reappeared, she did so with a small bottle of brandy and a cracked glass. She poured a healthy nip, sipped the elixir, and swished it around in her mouth before swallowing. "Makes great breath freshener."

Wells was frustrated. His indigestion had been bothering him for days now and the last thing he needed was this whore to waste his time. "Doris." Before he could utter another word, she interrupted with a biting remark, but it wasn't about him, rather one of her colleagues. "You're asking the wrong person, Sheriff."

"Mince said that Festus spent the night with you."

"Ha." She laughed. "What would he know? He spends all his time daydreaming about the missus that he doesn't see half as much as he thinks he hears."

Doris had enough. She decided that she was going to pack her bags and catch the afternoon stage. She didn't know where. Life at the Palace had been unkind to her. She aged, and her looks had faded. At least she still had her sense of humor, and that will be of some significance, but eventually the clients will stop coming around. She had seen it all before. In that situation a whore lowers her prices and then it's just a slippery slope to insignificance. She was on top of the slide, and she had been pushed, and it was that bloody whore next door who did it. Her voice was full of envy and spite. "Ask Tina."

The lawman shrugged his shoulders. "Who's Tina?"

"Came in on the stage a week ago. She came sashaying in here like she was the Queen of Texas." There was no stopping her now. He had to wait to let her empty her head of the rage that welled inside. "No taller than five feet. Pert and young. A smile that melts butter and a southern accent which is as fake as the innocence she portrays."

"Which room is hers?"

"Next door." She pointed nonchalantly.

Wells left the room, with Mince close behind. Doris fired off a parting quip, "you can tell that lunkhead to keep away from me. He had his chance, and he won't get another."

Her words were spat in anger, but the men weren't listening. They gave up on Doris and moved swiftly. The door slammed behind them.

A young woman answered the door to her room a minute later. She was as Doris described and despite the morning hour she was well dressed and presentable in a floral day dress. Her hair was in a bun on the top of her head, and her smile was enticing, yet cheeky.

"Miss?" The lawman was anxious.

"Miss. Evergreen. Tina Evergreen."

"Miss. Evergreen, my name is Sheriff Otis Wells, and I am looking for a man."

Her laughter was infectious, "aren't we all, Sheriff."

"Um, well. The man I am looking for is named Festus."

Her face turned red, and her temperature rose, as she turned, "that lug head, Sheriff."

He nodded and looked over her shoulder. "That very well could be the man I'm looking for."

"Well," she opened the door and beckoned them in with a wave of her hand, "get him out of my room. He's been snoring all night."

She pointed to the far corner of the room. Festus Rasmussen lay face down on the floor.

"Get me a bucket of water, Mince."

The barman hurried along.

Wells took the opportunity to question the witness to Festus' whereabouts. "How long has he been like this?"

She moved to the bedside table and sprayed some perfume into the air and walked through it.

"Since about eleven last night."

"Are you sure?"

"I might be a whore, but I'm not a fool or a liar."

"Miss. Evergreen, I'm only trying to establish his whereabouts."

She gestured angrily. "Drank and drank until he passed out. Claims to have no money, strange considering that he didn't buy a drink all night."

Wells nudged him with the toe of his boot. Nothing. He lifted his head by the hair. His forehead showed the implant of the floorboards. His stubble was filled with the drool that ran out of his mouth. There was no doubt about it. The smell was strong. Festus had passed out because of drink.

"You said he didn't buy a drink all night."

"They treated him as some sort of celebrity. He said that story repeatedly. Every time he did, he cried, and some sap would feel sorry for him and buy him another drink.

Mince stepped into the room with two buckets of water. "Figured you might have trouble waking him up."

"You could be right."

He rolled Festus on his back and accepted one bucket of water. He poured it from a height slowly on the drunk man's face. Instantly he showed signs of life, and he sat up. He tried to open his eyes and managed the feat, and without warning Mince swung the bucket back as far as he could and with force threw the contents into his face. The bald man smiled when Wells looked at him.

"Just trying to help, Sheriff."

Footsteps behind them brought Swan.

"Everything alright, Sheriff?"

Rasmussen laid back on the floor. His chest heaving. His breath ragged. Wells spoke to Mince.

"Did you see Festus leave the Palace?"

He shook his head. "Drank until late and staggered up the stairs with Tina at about ten."

"Before that?"

"Doris was all over him."

"What made Festus change his mind?"

"You've seen them, Sheriff, you make the comparison."

"That simple hey."

"That simple, Sheriff." Mince turned and left the room raising his eyebrows and smiling at the deputy.

It was silent for a while. Both lawmen looked at the prone figure as the working woman sashayed her way across the floor and ran her fingers along the side of Swan's cheek. "Aren't you the handsome one."

He stepped to the side, and she laughed.

The sheriff moved to the door. "As soon as Rasmussen comes around, take him to the back room of the courthouse."

"Yes, Sheriff."

"One more thing, Swan."

"Yes sir."

"Keep your hands to yourself."

Swan heard the footsteps of the big man disappear. The room fell silent. Miss. Evergreen, sat on the bed. She smiled and patted the mattress next to her, trying to entice the deputy. Nothing could be heard except the labored snoring of Festus Rasmussen.

CHAPTER 45

Wells paced back and forth along the worn floor of the law office. His thoughts were numerous. Swan held Festus Rasmussen in the back room of the courthouse. He would interview Rasmussen when he was sober enough to understand the questions he intended to ask. However, he had a feeling that the man was innocent of the murders and the rock throwing incident. It was a hunch, and he was usually right, however, he would follow due process. Meanwhile there was some figuring out and work to do. He needed to get his thoughts clear in his head. He rubbed his stomach. "This blasted indigestion."

Poole sat at the desk scribbling on a pad. His mood was pensive. He was considering the state of play and was at a loss as to how to respond. He didn't know what to say, and anything he said would have been inadequate, besides, he would have interrupted the sheriff.

Wells continued to pace back and forth. The rock throwing incident had baffled him. Was it the same people who robbed Cloverfield in the alley? The assault in the alley provided evidence of a random attack, while this was much more personal. The incident last night occurred when the star witness for the defense arrived in town. Who was the target of the attack? Cloverfield assured the lawman that no one knew of the expert witness' arrival, and that the attack was directed squarely at him. Wells tended to agree with the lawyer. It was a hunch he had, but he ran with it. Was the person who threw the rock the same person who killed Hammond and Johns? If so, why? There was much to figure out.

At best he could reason that two people were murdered. The lawyer was attacked, and the man had an alibi. Two whores and a bartender had vouched that Rasmussen was drunk and never left the building. If indeed Rasmussen passed out before midnight, then that was well before the men were murdered. Two whores alone probably wouldn't be believed, but the addition of Mince as a witness would nullify any attack on the whore's credibility. He was known as a judicious and prompt individual and was respected for his forthright manner. Indeed, it has been said that the man didn't know how to lie. Faced with the evidence, the law needed to look in another direction. But where? The citizens of Rocksprings had enough of the violence and would soon demand answers to their questions. Sure, they respected the sheriff, but respect wasn't enough when people were fearful. They often acted irrationally. The need to feel safe was natural, and the tendency to lash out at others was equally so.

Wells paused before the window and looked to the east. What he saw surprised him. It was Majorie Jayne Bland, the wife of the butcher. She was tall and thin. Her long black hair disheveled, and unkempt. Her face was long and gaunt. She walked haphazardly, as if in a daze. A shawl wrapped around her shoulders. A look of desperation in her eyes. She was quite different from the woman who locked herself away from the outside world. She headed directly for the jail.

"Poole, you won't believe who is heading here."

Sensing his boss's urgency, he stood and moved across to the window. He whistled in disbelief. "I haven't seen Mrs. Bland in years."

Wells moved across to the door, and without saying a word opened it and ushered Mrs. Bland in. His voice was suspicious and inquisitive. "Please sit, Marjorie." He sat her down and moved across to the other side of the desk. "Throw another log on the fire, Deputy and bring Mrs. Bland a mug of coffee."

She closed her eyes and breathed deeply. When she opened them, she stared at the lawman. "Please don't call me Mrs. Bland. My maiden name, as you well know, is Tracey. Either call me Miss. Tracey or Marjorie. I want nothing to do with that man."

Wells nodded, "sure Marjorie." It was then that Wells recalled the butcher not being in court that morning, and along with Hammond, his absence had intrigued him.

Poole handed the woman a mug of coffee, and picked up the pad and pencil and began recording the conversation.

Her voice was weak. "Thanks."

"Majorie. Are you all right? Would you like me to get Von Klaus?"

"If I wanted the doctor, it would be him that I seek help from, not the law."

He nodded in agreement, but he still intended to get Von Klaus. "What can the law do for you Mrs. Bland?" He apologized at once. "Sorry, Miss. Tracey."

She ignored him and held the mug of coffee thoughtfully between her hands before blowing on it and taking a sip. "It's Thomas, Sheriff. I fear he has done something awful. In fact, I am convinced he is guilty of a heinous act."

He leaned close. "What makes you say that?"

She lifted her head and smiled wanly. "I know everything, Sheriff. The debt, and his rendezvous with his floozies. I know it all, and I know something terrible happened last night."

"Do you know what happened last night, Marjorie?"

She shook her head and closed her eyes. "I only know what I saw."

He was intrigued and leaned closer while Poole wrote feverishly. "What was it you saw?"

Her eyes were darting left and right. She looked over her shoulder to the door as if expecting someone.

"It's okay Marjorie. You are safe. Please tell me what you saw."

She sighed and persisted. "We are in debt, rather, Thomas is. He owes the Favell's money and is in debt to the bank. He is unable to borrow any more money, and his payments have been late. He is in danger of losing the business."

Wells wanted to push her but thought it better to let the story flow naturally.

She continued. "He thinks I know nothing, but I know everything." She laughed and smiled at this. "I know everything, Sheriff. Thomas left home late last night and returned sometime later covered in blood. I fear he has done something awful."

"Are you positive?"

"Yes, Sheriff."

His voice was low. "Marjorie, two people were murdered last night."

She lowered her head and began crying. "Who were they?"

"The newspaperman, Hammond, and Wiley Johns."

She knew Johns and only heard about Hammond. From all accounts he wasn't a nice man, still he had no need to be murdered. Poole interjected. "Those cuts were expertly performed. Deep and clean, Sheriff."

He thought, just the type of cuts a butcher could make. Wells stood. "Where is your husband now?"

She stared at him pleadingly, "please don't call him that."

"Marjorie, if what you told me is true, then I need to find Thomas before he decides to hurt anyone else."

"When I left home, he was sitting in the chair passed out drunk."

That explains why he wasn't in court, thought the lawman. It had all come together, quicker than he could have imagined and it all made sense.

"Poole," Wells stood, and took his Greener from the gun rack above his head.

"Yes, Sheriff."

"Stay here with Miss. Tracey."

"You can't be serious about going after Bland by yourself."

"We're stretched thin. Swan is at the courthouse, and I need you here to protect the prisoner and Miss. Tracey.

I'll find Bland. I'll need to talk with him."

"What if he won't talk?"

The woman interjected. "Sheriff, Thomas won't give in. He'd rather die and face God's wrath than the ridicule of the townsfolk."

Wells nodded and moved across the floor and exited through the door.

CHAPTER 46

Thomas Bland was consumed with a feeling of dread. The fear of being caught was more powerful than any concern he had for the lives of the men he took. He stood at the kitchen sink, washed his hands, and splashed water on his face to clear the cobwebs. He was still intoxicated. He closed his eyes and recalled butchering Hammond and Johns. He smiled, pleased with his butchering skills. He cussed Hammond for scratching him. He made a fatal error, his lack of stealth the cause for the scratches. Lighting a cigar, he moved into the back room for another change of clothes. He walked past his wife's room. He had more important things to worry about than that useless old wench as he referred to her. Even though she wasn't old or a wench it was Bland's attempt at shaping his wife's personality. He was halfway down the hall when he heard a heavy knock on the door and the commanding words behind them. "Thomas Bland, it's Sheriff Wells. Open this door."

Bland scurried into the sitting room and retrieved his Henry rifle. He stepped lightly back to the hall fearing being heard. The lawman's voice boomed again. "Bland. I know you're in there."

Silence, he didn't move. The lawman rattled the door again and tried to open it.

"What do you want, Sheriff?"

"Talk is all. Just talk."

"I've got nothing to say to you, vamoose."

"Can't do that, Thomas. We need to talk."

"What for?"

Wells was not used to such confrontation, and perhaps he could have used a little more tact, but the situation necessitated a swift conclusion. A passerby had already become aware of the scene and no doubt there would be a passel of onlookers before too long. "The murder of Wiley Johns and Miles Hammond."

The lawman's inexperience in such matters became obvious when Bland fired through the door. A bullet hit the door knob and penetrated the thin veneer of the door and caught Wells in the foot. He cussed and stepped backward. Losing his footing and tumbling down the stairs.

Bland moved swiftly to the kitchen window and saw the prone figure of the Sheriff. He broke the glass and aimed at Wells, who rolled over and fired a barrel of the Greener at the window. There was a scream from inside. Bland had been hit. Shards of glass from the broken window became embedded in his face. Blood oozed from the cuts.

"You bastard." Screamed Bland. "You rotten, weasel faced, limp backed son of a bitch. I'm going to kill you if it's the last thing I do."

Wells hobbled to the wall and leaned against it.

"Time to surrender, Thomas."

"I am not surrendering."

"There's no chance of escape. Surrender and I will see that you get a fair trial."

"I'm not hanging for killing that no-good reporter and the old man."

Wells leaned against the wall. His indigestion troubled him, and his wounded foot also caused him some grief, he breathed heavily and closed his eyes for a moment. For what seemed an eternity there was silence, and Wells grew apprehensive when he realized that

Bland could easily have escaped through the back door. He was silly to come after the man by himself. He needed to surround the building and hem the killer in. He was contemplating his next move when he heard the friendly voice of Poole, and his distant yell. "I have Bland covered from the back, Sheriff."

He didn't know how, but he knew Poole would not disobey an order unless there were solid reasons to do so. There was only one lawman, Swan, to guard two prisoners in two separate places. He wanted to know how this could have been achieved, but now was not the right time, instead he shifted his attention to Thomas 'the butcher' Bland. "Why did you do it, Thomas? Why did you kill Hammond and Johns?"

The butcher heard Poole. He was trapped and the only way out was to shoot his way out or die trying. He had already decided that he wouldn't hang. Not at all. He had watched a man hang and he lost all control of his bodily functions. It was a public spectacle. All the public could talk about for weeks afterward was the embarrassment of this public display. He would rather be filled with lead than suffer the indignity.

He ignored the question. "I have a hostage, Sheriff."

"Who?"

"My wife. I will kill her if you don't back away. Tell Poole to move around the front. Stand where I can see you both. Leave me a horse in the alley, and I'll ride away."

On both sides of the house the lawmen smiled and laughed. It was Poole who spoke. "You have no hostage, Bland."

"Don't think I'm bluffing, Deputy."

Wells persisted. "You're not bluffing, though a little misunderstood."

Poole laughed. "Check your wife's room."

They heard a scurry inside. His heavy booted feet stomped across the floor. A door slammed, and he cussed. "Where is she? What have you done with her?"

The sheriff spoke again. The constant back and forth was irritating the butcher. "She told us everything. If I spoke to Denning, he would confirm that you owed the bank money. When I speak to the Favell's I have no doubt they will likewise confirm that you owe them money. As best I could figure, Thomas, is that you killed Hammond and Johns for monetary gains.

Poole said, "how much did you get?"

Wells asked, "was it worth ending the lives of two innocent people?"

The sheriff heard voices and the scuff of boots behind him. He didn't turn. There was no point in trying to move the folk of Rocksprings on. It was just too exciting. If Wells turned, he would have seen at least twenty people. They were a motley lot. Some were standing in the open, others were hiding behind water troughs, and one brave soul was sitting on their bay seventy yards away. The onlookers jostled for prime viewing position. Silence. They wanted to hear what was said and observe every action.

"No one is innocent, Sheriff?"

It was Wells who took over the talking. "What about Marjorie?"

"What about her?" His voice was harsh and dry. His tone was condemning.

"What did Marjorie do to deserve being treated so harshly?"

"None of your business."

"You're surrounded, Thomas. Come peaceably. There is no escape for you."

Bland began sobbing. There was no way out. He removed a piece of glass from his face and screamed in pain. He was doomed. Regardless of the door he exited. He would be cut down by the lawmen's guns. Still the front or the back door were his only options. He moved across to the window and peered through the broken glass. He aimed the Henry rifle at the man on horseback and fired. The shot was wide, but it was fatal nonetheless as the bay collapsed to the ground and let out a plaintive cry before gargling on its blood and dying shortly after. The man on the horse scurried to the other side of the road as a slug hit the earth three feet behind him. Another slug burned his britches and caused him to holler. The onlookers, well-secured in their strongholds couldn't help but laugh. Once he was safe, the man rubbed his backside. He was bleeding, though he would live to be the butt of the townsfolk's jokes for years to come.

Bland leaned his back against the wall and felt for a piece of glass in his face and pulled it free. Blood ran down his face. He was in a world of pain. Breathing heavy, he considered his options, and they were few. He wouldn't face the gallows. There was a chance that he would be sent to prison where there was a possibility of escape. Yes, there is always a possibility. The situation was hopeless. He had no choice but to surrender. Faced with the time of death, he began sobbing. Why? Why him? He didn't deserve it. Self-pity is such an unattractive trait. Hope, there is always hope. Isn't that what good Christians believed. Without hope there was nothing. The sheriff's voice cut through his thoughts.

"That's attempted murder, Bland." Wells yelled as he realized the extent of the pain in his foot.

"What a fool." he muttered to himself, as he reloaded.

Meanwhile, Poole looked through the back window. There was a gap in the curtain, and he could see along the hallway to the faintly lit room at the end of the hall. Bland would have to traverse the hallway to reach the back door. He needed to take the attention away from his compatriot, and he devised a plan. The deputy rapped the butt of his rifle against the window, and it shattered. The noise startled the butcher and brought him around. He screamed in fury and approached the sound of the noise. By this time Poole was ready and when the hulking frame came into view he fired. A bullet hummed out of the long rifle and made contact. The slug slapped into the meaty flesh of Bland's thigh.

"Arrgh. You bastard." He screamed.

The deputy fired again, but the wounded man was quick and managed to scramble back into the kitchen as the slug kicked splinters out of the floorboard near his feet.

Silence.

"Poole, are you alright?" The sheriff screamed.

"Fine, Sheriff, just giving Thomas something else to think about. "I winged him, Sheriff. Hit him in the thigh. I've got the back secured."

"Did you hear that, Thomas? You're trapped. There's no way out."

His sobbing grew louder. Lying on the kitchen floor bleeding from a gaping wound on his thigh. Glass in his face. He was finished. With the courage of a dying man, content to pass from the land of the living to be judged on the course of his actions he managed to right himself with the aid of a chair. "I'm coming out, Sheriff, but I am going down fighting."

"Not that way. Lay your gun down and walk outside with your hands in the air."

"I can't do it, Wells. You know me, it's all or nothing."

"Doesn't have to be that way."

Wells could hear movement inside. There was a slow plod on the floor, and the door squeaked as it opened. Wells lay as flat as he could. The Greener pointing toward the space Bland would have to step into when he came outside. The hinges of the door squeaked long and slow. Poole couldn't see, but he decided to add some haste and fired some steady rounds into the wall and the floor. This had the desired effect. Bland stepped into the space hurriedly and began firing wildly at the onlookers across the street. He wasn't aiming and the slugs were wild. Wells lay without being seen and he aimed the Greener and fired. The shot hit Bland in the left shoulder and side. It spun him around so that his startled face and front were exposed. The sheriff fired again, and the pellets ripped Bland's face and neck apart. He stumbled in an awkward and bloody mess, falling to his right down the stairs. His body came to rest face first in the dirt.

239

CHAPTER 47

The following morning an inquiry was held into the shooting of Thomas Bland. The inquest was conducted by Judge McBean in his chambers at the courthouse. Present were McBean, Sheriff Wells, Deputy Poole, and Marjorie Bland, nee Tracey. Purcell was also present, as he represented the state, and his assistance was required to verify the findings. McBean read every statement for the second time. He had no doubt that the lawmen had acted appropriately, he just wanted to be transparent and ensure that since he was in town for the trial that he would make the most of his presence. Besides, Wells wanted his name cleared of any wrongdoing, in case an ally of Bland came forward to complain about his death. This was unlikely, but he was a judicious officer of the law.

McBean removed his glasses and wiped his eyes. "Miss. Tracey, I have read your statement and I'm sorry for what you have endured over the years, but I trust and hope that your life takes a different course now that you are free from the clutches of this man."

She smiled. She wasn't seeking sympathy, nor did she want it. She could have easily stated as much, but she knew that McBean meant well and was not condescending in extending his condolences. It was true that she was free of her husband's physical grasp, but he had left some mental scarring which would take some maneuvering.

McBean continued. "Purcell. Miss. Tracey has filed a petition for her marriage to Thomas Bland to be declared invalid. As part of this petition, she also requests her maiden name be used in place of her married name. The court grants permission of course. Make haste and ensure the necessary arrangements."

His voice was sincere. "It shall be done at once, Your Honor." He turned to the woman. "Miss. Tracey, I will see to it myself, free of charge. I will be in touch with the necessary paperwork."

She managed to smile. "Thank you for your kindness, Mr. Purcell, it is appreciated."

Wells moved, and pain shot from his foot up his leg.

"Are you okay, Sheriff?" McBean asked sincerely.

"Fine." He said between clenched teeth, "just fine."

"You need rest. Von Klaus told me himself. Use your crutches when you walk, and don't overexert yourself."

Wells laughed heartily. "Between you, the doctor, Poole, Swan, and the wife I have received lots of advice which I intend to adhere to. I will be making camp at the office while the young deputies do all the running around."

"Don't get too comfortable," McBean joked, "you will be required in court over the next few days. Court will resume at 10:00 am tomorrow morning. But that's not why we are here."

There was a pause. There was a feeling of satisfaction. Of contentment, but they knew that the next few days were vital in determining the outcome of the case against Noble.

"May I say a few words?" Miss. Tracey's voice was polite, and her request was gentle.

"Of course, Miss. Tracey."

She cleared her throat. "I would like to thank Sheriff Wells, and Deputy Poole for taking my complaints against my husband, oh how I hate to use that word, seriously. I know they had cause to suspect him of a most heinous offense, yet they acted swiftly and were professional in every regard. I owe them a debt of gratitude. Mr. Purcell, thank you for your assistance. It is a most respectful gesture, and I cannot express my happiness enough. Thank you, Judge, for being earnest in your response. The sooner I clear this mess up, the better I will feel."

McBean lowered his head and his voice. "If you don't mind me asking, Miss. Tracey, what are your plans for the future?"

"I have been held captive by a loveless man in a loveless marriage. I have been confined by brute force and the threat of violence on my person. I am free, Your Honor and I intend to remain that way. I have a sister in Austin who I haven't seen in many years. I will be leaving in a matter of days, and I will never return. Mr. Purcell, I will give you her address for correspondence."

The room fell silent. There was nothing left to say, so McBean cleared his throat and handed down his finding. "This inquiry was held to determine whether the actions of Sheriff Wells and Deputy Poole in the death of Thomas Bland were justified. After consideration of the evidence, including written and verbal statements, the death of Thomas Bland was justified and carried out within the realms of power as entrusted to officers of the law. This inquiry is concluded."

CHAPTER 48

Festus Rasmussen was released from the courthouse late on the afternoon of the death of the butcher. He was held under guard by Judge McBean. Poole, entrusted with the care and protection of the prisoner and Miss. Tracey, quickly scribbled a note, and handed it to Buck Dempsey, a strapping young man who worked at the livery stable. He just happened to be walking past with a package that he received from the post. It was some linen for his mamma. She worked as a seamstress, out of her home, three miles east of Rocksprings. Sensing the urgency of the request he hastened along and carried out the errand. McBean read the message and removed the Colt .45 that sat in the top draw of his desk. "Thanks son," your duty to the state of Texas has been fulfilled." He stood and shook the lad's hand. Dempsey was a proud young man and stood straight. "Is there anything else I can do?" he asked, keen to offer more assistance. "Take care of your mamma, Buck." He patted the boy on the shoulder and ushered him out the door. Time was of the essence. Within minutes, Swan had been relieved by

McBean, and Poole by Swan. The exchange had been swift.

Festus Rasmussen was advised not to leave town until the sheriff had questioned him. He had no plans to leave, not yet anyway. Deadeye Dave was getting buried the following day, and he wasn't leaving town until he said his last goodbyes. He also needed to talk to the banker, Joe Denning, about selling the mine. Now that he was the single owner of the mines, and with a penchant for drink and whores rather than hard work, it would be best to take the money and leave the county. He would go west. Everyone wanted to go east, but not Festus. The stories from the grand cities attracted his youthful spirit. Washington and New York. City life. High class whores and fine whiskey. The notions enticed him. Yes sir, such temptations would have been enough to lure him, but Santa Fe was his destination and he let everyone know it. It was time to leave. He decided his future while lying on the cold wooden floor of the back room of the courthouse. It was a small, dark, and cool room, without a window and natural light. The perfect place to hold a suspect.

Doris spent the afternoon packing her belongings. She had made up her mind to catch the stage. She didn't know where she was going, but the scene was set. The drama of the last six weeks or so were bearable, and she managed herself well enough, but she was worn out. The entrance of the young whore, Tina Evergreen, made life unbearable. Her position at the top of the tree was pulled from under her. It wasn't Tina's fault. She was young and pretty like she had been years before. That's all there was to it. It was time to leave the profession, find a husband and become a boring old housewife, or a miserable spinster. Neither of the options appealed to her. Still, she had to make up her mind and whatever she chose to do had to be far enough away from Rocksprings so that her previous profession would not jeopardize her prospects.

Owen Restful was lying at rest in the back room of Cloverfield's residence when Von Klaus and McBean entered the room. The lawyer looked edgy and nervous. He needed time to prepare the expert witness and another day was crucial if they had any chance of getting Noble off the murder charge. Restful had been coached by

Cloverfield, and the witness was acting the part. It was a shameful display. Von Klaus erred, as most doctors do to prevent a lawsuit, on the side of caution and decided that the man needed another day of rest. He went on to state, quite determinedly, that "any more rest would be a waste of life, and there were more important things to do than to nurse a grown man."

McBean smiled at this remark and stepped aside to let a restless Von Klaus pass. The doctor had not worked so hard in a long time. He preferred to be sitting by the light in his office reading rather than running around the countryside, as he said, "tending to people's feelings, rather than their physical ailments." It is obvious, though it must be said, that his bedside manner was a little terse at times. McBean eyed Cloverfield and Restful. They were a foolish pair. In his estimation, the defense was losing the trial, and this was a final effort by a desperate lawyer and a pseudo professional quack to regain some respectability. Individually they were tolerable to a degree, as a pair they would be insufferable. The judge smiled; what he was about to say he was going to say all along. He just wanted to see the charade unfold before him. "Court is postponed to the day after tomorrow. There are funerals to be had and statements to be obtained. The law is stretched thin, and priorities must be made."

Cloverfield nodded and uttered a sigh of relief. Restful looked at the lawyer as if to ask, "can I have a drink now?" The star witness soon jumped out of bed when the judge left. He was anxious and beginning to shake. He needed a drink. The lawyer watched Restful. The shakes were getting worse. He was gaunt and pale. Still, there was a job to do and that was to convince the jury that his client had been insane when he landed the blow that killed Jake Jenkins.

CHAPTER 49

Deadeye Dave was buried mid-morning. The crowd was sizable, but the mourners were few. Festus Rasmussen stood at the foot of the grave as the pine box was lowered in the ground. He shed a tear. Tina Evergreen stood next to him. She looped her arm between his. She spoke no soothing words. Shed no tears. In fact, she was bored. She did everything for a purpose. She was calculating and conniving. She used others to satisfy her needs, and that need was money. That is why she was standing next to Rasmussen, the smelly big man. She wore black and a veil so no one could see her smile. Tina Evergreen had found a place that time almost forgot. Where time passed slowly, and news of the outside world never made it. She had only been in town a week, but she could see a future for a bright girl like her, at least for a few years as she earned her wealth. She has already caught the attention of Mr. Favell, the owner of the Western Palace. It wouldn't be long before she could ensnare him with her feminine wiles. Life was looking up for Tina Evergreen.

"The Lord knows thy secrets," bellowed Reverend Thaddeus Blair. He was a large man, standing six foot four inches. He carried too much weight, but his command of the Holy Bible was second to none and his ability to change tone and pitch while delivering a sermon was what led people to believe that he was preaching to them personally. His face was pale, yet his eyes were warm. His smile was welcoming and the respect he had from the people of Rocksprings and the surrounding county was genuine. He was a likable fellow, a little too pious at times, but just the right man for the job of tending to the spiritual needs of the citizens in these troubled times.

It was a time to remind people of their duty to one another. These were immoral times. He continued. "Let no man speak ill of his brother and sister. It is not your duty to judge, that responsibility belongs to God and God alone. Instead, reach out a helping hand to a neighbor. Offer a kind word to a loved one or a stranger. Good deeds do not go unrewarded. They are deposits in your spiritual bank. Your moral wealth is at the heart of your relations with others. Do not let greed corrupt your soul.

You must make the right choice. Lust is a lurid temptation. The devil tempts us all. He infects our soul with the fulfillment of desire. He infects our mind with lust. The dust of man, the simplicity of life, and the durability of faith go hand in hand. We are not innocent lambs sacrificed to God. We are his sons and daughters on a path of righteousness. Our faith is tested. Our spiritual strength is challenged. Our morality is questioned. When the sun sets on our mortality, we will be called to testify before God. What will you say? Judgment day. JUDGMENT DAY." His voice rose to a crescendo. "All that is holy and just dwells in all of us. We are kind and forgiving. We seek no restitution for our deeds except eternal salvation. Life is simple. Our instructions are clear. Only those who live a sinful life fear death. It is a courteous displeasure to measure man against man, thus, man must be measured against the holy tenets of faith. We are sinners. We must repent. We are not without fault. The good book teaches us many lessons about love. In 1 Corinthians 13:13 it is stated that *'hope, faith and love abide, yet out of these three, the greatest of these is love.'* The deceivers and the deceived walk among us. The unholy and the unjust move stealthily between the shadows. Yet here we stand. On the dust that created Adam. The son of sons. A sinner. Tempted by desire. Tempted by lust, just like you. Just like me. We must not yield. Our spirit is precious. It is water to a dying man. Make a stand. Which way will you lean? Will your soul be blown away by the ill and crooked wind that has settled over Rocksprings, or will you follow the path of righteousness? The decision is yours."

He paused before opening the bible and reciting the Lord's Prayer.

"Ashes to ashes and dust to dust." Amen.

The mourners. No, that is not the right word. The attendees repeated the last word. "Amen."

The crowd relaxed and mingled. Many of them lined up to pay their respects to Festus, before out of duty to Reverend Blair. Soon enough the crowd thinned out and all that remained was Festus standing silently, a little morose and questioning. Tina Evergreen still looped her arm through his and was getting restless. She looked over her shoulder. Men were anxious to drink, that meant there was money to be made. She was saved from her boredom by Festus. His voice was low, and she could tell that he had been crying. "You can go now. I need to speak to the reverend."

"Whatever," she said and waved him aside. Picking the hems of her dress, up to prevent them dragging in the dust of Adam, she made her way down the rise to town.

Festus approached Reverend Blair, with a shuffling gait. "Excuse me, Reverend."

The big man looked up from his bible. He was always the last one to leave a burial or a wedding. The guests and the mourners lingered just for this occasion. It was at such times that people felt their mortality and sought out the reverend's company.

His voice was reassuring. "The dear departed was a close friend of yours?" It was more of a statement than a question. Regardless, Festus didn't respond either way. He stumbled over his words and had difficulty getting the thoughts right.

"Take your time my son. Death of a loved one can be difficult to manage."

His voice was plaintive. "Is stealing a sin?"

"Yes son. It is. Stealing in a sin."

"What about killing? Is murder a sin?"

"Killing is a heinous crime, and a serious sin."

"What about lying?"

"Lying can be a sin, not always, but it most certainly can be."

"How do you get rid of sin?"

"You can't get rid of sin my child; you can only repent."

Festus was in over his head. The words didn't make sense to him. "Repent?"

"Repent means to express sincere remorse and/or regret for things you have done." Blair watched the man closely. He could read a face like a psalm. He knew the man was troubled. He had never seen the man in church yet knew he had been in the area for some years now. "Is there something you'd like to confess?" He considered the word 'confess' and rephrased the question. "Is there some sin you'd like to admit to?"

Festus Rasmussen was troubled. He hadn't lived a noble and honest life. He had stolen and killed before. He got drunk many times, laid with whores and took great delight in fighting. It seemed to him that all the pleasurable things were sins. Just last night he sinned. Why this very morning he had wicked thoughts, and he knew thoughts were sins. He didn't know why; he just knew they were.

Reverend Blair stepped closer and made eye contact with Rasmussen and laid a hand on his shoulder. "The Lord is your shepherd. It is not too late; it is never too late to seek forgiveness." He sensed that the man had given all he was able or willing to at this time. Blair patted him twice on the shoulder and moved on.

He felt alone. He missed Jenkins, but he missed Deadeye more than ever. It was the latter's practicality and wit he missed. He was also a great storyteller. Stories of life on the land and during the Civil War entertained and intrigued him. Being illiterate he relied on his companion to paint his world with words. He most certainly did that. Out of respect for the dead he threw some dirt on the pine box and moved on.

A skinny and wiry tough old fellow by the name of Ernest shrugged his shoulders, leaned off the shovel and began filling up the hole. He often wondered at times what people would say about him when he passed. At times, the thought occupied his mind for days on end, but he was feeling a little gnarly today. He had just found out that Doris bought a ticket on the stage and was planning to leave Rocksprings forever.

CHAPTER 50

Wells, Poole, and Swan sat around the desk at the office. They could hear Noble snoring. The prisoner did little else except sleep and read the bible. He was at peace with himself. No doubt, the regular visits with Millie Tippet eased his conscience. After the threats made against Swan, he was issued an ultimatum by Wells. It was simple 'apologize to Swan, who was acting under orders, or the visiting rights of Miss. Tippet would be revoked.' It was that simple. Begrudgingly Noble apologized. The outburst was a blight against his character, and he believed that the incident would be mentioned in court, but not a word had been spoken.

Noble had spent an hour with his lawyer and doctor Restful, under the scrutiny of the lawmen. They were afforded as much privacy as was allowed. They spent a little over an hour together. During this time, they confirmed their approach. Restful obtained some background information about how Noble was raised and how he had been treated by his parents. He also considered his engagement to the whore relevant, yet he wasn't sure how. It would all make sense in the light of day, after consideration was given to the occasion. The truth could be bent to suit a narrative and it was his job to do so. He was being paid handsomely to do so.

Miss. Tippet had spent an hour visiting with Noble that very afternoon. They read the bible. Noble liked the psalms, and they spent time discussing them. It was like they were old friends, yet Swan was adamant that he knew better. He went as far as to mention to Wells and Poole five minutes ago that he believed that they were in love. That was right before an unsettling silence settled upon them. It was a strange feeling because for once a sedate and peaceful air had settled over Rocksprings.

Swan rubbed his hands together and blew into them. "Trial restarts again tomorrow. It'll all be over in a few days. Life will get back to normal."

"And I'll be grateful for it," replied the other deputy.

"You're forgetting something," added Wells, "we still don't know who threw the rock through the window at Cloverfield."

"I am not forgetting," muttered Poole, "I'm just stumped. Seems we've discussed this so many times and are no closer to figuring out who the culprit is."

The sheriff continued, "well, I doubt it was Festus. He was held and questioned. There were at least three witnesses that could vouch for his whereabouts."

"Why the lawyer?" Poole was perplexed but kept his train of thought. "I mean, why throw a rock through this window? Isn't Noble the murderer of Jenkins? Why would CC be the main target?"

Swan added. "I'm thinking that there's no rock thrower." The other lawmen looked at him, perplexed. Swan held up his hand to warn them off. "Hear me out. CC gets drunk, stumbles home, and has a fall. Now he is a smart man and decides to use this to his advantage. That is to draw the focus away from Noble. It works for a time, but then Hammond writes a series of damning articles about his incompetence and wham, there is the rock throwing incident in which his star witness gets hurt."

"A fall would explain his injuries," mused Poole, who was warming to the idea that Swan was onto something. He continued, but this time to the sheriff. "Do you think it would be past Cloverfield to concoct the rock throwing incident?"

Wells stood, limped across to the fire and refilled his mug with coffee, and returned to sit at his chair. His injury wasn't that bad. The bullet hit the bridge of his foot and skimmed across the surface. It was painful, but not life threatening. Von Klaus had done a fair job cleaning it up. "I can't say for certain that he wouldn't do it."

"Perhaps Swan is onto something." Pushed Poole.

Wells leaned back in his chair. The lawmen had asked around, and had interviewed most folk, but the information was the same. No one knew a thing about either the mugging or the rock throwing incident. The sheriff changed the topic of conversation.

"They buried Bland this afternoon after Deadeye. Marjorie wanted to keep it quiet. She figured her husband didn't deserve to have anyone attend the service. She didn't even go. She simply instructed the reverend to say a few words."

"What about Hammond and Johns?"

"Hammond will be buried tomorrow afternoon and Johns the day after. Poor old Ernest can't dig any faster. The poor old bloke is about plumb tuckered out."

Poole said, "what do you think makes a man lose the plot like that? I mean, he was a good butcher. Meat was always fresh. His wife was beautiful when they married. Why would he treat her that way? Why Hammond? Why Johns? The old bloke never hurt a soul."

Swan rubbed his eyes and stood. "Too many questions. That's the problem with life, there are many more questions than there are answers. See you in the morning." He left the senior lawmen alone.

Poole moved behind Wells and urged him forward. "Hobble home, Sheriff. I'm on duty tonight."

He obeyed the instruction, winced as he stood and reached for the crutches. "Goodnight Wilson."

CHAPTER 51

Cletus Cloverfield, lawyer of the accused, Timothy Noble, and self-proclaimed man of the people was getting frustrated. His coaching of Owen Restful was progressing slowly. The man was too unsteady. He was a wreck. He had been attuned to functioning on alcohol for so long that there just wasn't time to detox enough so that he could focus. It was impossible to be granted more time, so he had to work out a solution. He paced back and forth. Cursing and snarling his predicament. He wanted to escape and disappear forever. His ideals of winning the case and making a name for himself were fading rapidly. He cursed Hammond who used his meek power to defame and ridicule him. When he found out that Hammond had been murdered, he smiled. Cletus Cloverfield was a cold son of a gun. He came across as this jovial and laughable giant, but he was insidious and as calculating as any crook. He lit a cigar and stepped outside. The fresh air did nothing to ease his temper. He soon realized the error of his ways and hastened inside only to find the doctor swinging on a bottle of brandy.

"I'm ready now." He stood and cleared his throat.

The lawyer looked startled.

"I see the look in your eye my friend. You appear confused."

He stepped forward. "Give me the bottle."

Restful smiled and handed the brandy over. "I function best with liquor, Cletus. Don't make me go cold turkey. It won't work. A nip every now and then. That is the remedy. The trick is to keep the bottle away from me. I am a child and respond to positive rewards. The promise of a drink is good enough for me."

CC took the bottle and eyed the man carefully. One drop of brandy had changed the man's demeanor. He looked more capable. Oh, he still looked terrible, but decidedly stronger and more capable. He decided to test the doctor's theory. "We will go back over the questions and your responses, then I will give you another drink."

"Excellent."

"It is late, so then we will go to bed. I can give you a drink with breakfast, and no more until your testimony has been concluded. After that you can drink as much as you like."

"Very well my friend. That sounds perfectly fine."

The next hour was productive. They went through some of the questions that would be asked and some of the possible objections. Restful sounded perfectly legitimate. He held himself together. Gone was the shaking, and the nervousness he displayed. His hands were steady and his gaze more determined. He looked worn and tired which he could easily put down to travel and a recent mild sickness.

The lights went out soon thereafter, but not before he was allowed one more drink. The host locked the door and hid the bottle of brandy in his room. The guest fell asleep easily, while Cloverfield lay unmoving, staring at the ceiling into the darkness. He had fluffed the trial from the start. It wasn't one big thing, rather a series of misses. It was an objection he didn't make, a cross-examination question he didn't ask, and or an issue he didn't push. He would be making his opening statement tomorrow morning and then he would call his main witness. Success of the case depended on the validity of Restful's testimony. He had to be believable, he just had to. He ran over his opening statement, of which only the key points were written down. He simply had no time to write it properly, besides when on his game he relished the freedom to ad lib. He simply needed to be at his best.

His thoughts changed to the rock-throwing incident. He believed that it was someone either from his past seeking revenge or a message from one of the deceased friends. The message was clear. Back off. When he spoke to Wells, whom he trusted, he was informed that they simply had no evidence, apart from the rock and the misspelled note. The only genuine suspect was Festus Rasmussen, but he had an air-tight alibi. He wasn't overly concerned about his safety. If his life was in danger, then there was plenty of opportunity to carry out the threat. But now, in the early hours of the morning on the biggest day of his life every minor issue became magnified. He thought too much. He became scared and then defiant. He hated the world because he had no solutions to the problems he faced, but then when he finally found a solution, he fell into a fitful sleep.

CHAPTER 52

"Your Honor. I would like to remind the court that the standard of proof in a criminal trial is beyond reasonable doubt. That means simply," he waved a finger at the jury as he moved closer and stood before them, "that there must be no doubt that the accused intended to kill, that is, murder the deceased Jake Jenkins. NO DOUBT. His intention must be clear, that is formulated prior to the conflict, and or established in the heat of the moment by a reasonable and sane man." Some members of the jury were startled, quite simply because they didn't like being pointed at.

"I would also like to remind the court that it is not the role of the defense to prove the accused innocent. The burden of proof lies with the prosecution. Ladies and gentlemen," he opened his arms wide as if he were welcoming a loved one, "this means that the prosecution," once again he pointed at Purcell, "MUST prove the accused formed the necessary intent to murder." That is the legal standard that must be met." His tone changed, "we live in the land of freedom.

Democracy and the rule of law underpin the freedoms we enjoy today. Freedom of speech. The freedom of religion. The right to bear arms. The right to vote. We are a blessed people. America is a beacon for the world. A light on a rocky cove for a wayward ship. A glass of water to a man dying of thirst. My client, one Timothy Noble, stands accused of murder. That is intentionally planning to kill another, and if we did not live in this country, our country, America, then he would have been declared guilty and hung from the nearest tree."

Cloverfield was loose with the facts. People were still being hanged from trees. Justice was still swift in some places. Questions weren't asked. Nobody talked. In places like Hackberry and Telegraph there was no official law, and people took matters into their own hands.

"The fundamental belief of the legal system is that the accused is innocent until proven guilty. Such a noble concept is the foundation of a just legal system." He paused for a moment to consider the delivery of his next point. "It is the defense's contention that significant doubt will be cast upon the motivations of the accused.

How? Expert testimony will be presented to the court that the accused did not have the wherewithal to formulate the necessary *mens rea*. That is the criminal intent to murder."

Some of the jury were impressed. They were hearing words that they have never heard before. CC knew exactly what he was doing, and just maybe he wasn't as incapable as some of them were led to believe.

"In consideration of the evidence thus tendered to court I ask that you consider the testimony to be presented with the genuine respect and dignity it deserves." He paused again and sensed he had them hanging on every word he continued. "Have you ever acted spontaneously? Without thinking? Of course, you have, as have I. Have you ever lashed out in anger without consideration of your actions, or the unintended consequences of those actions? Why do we act in such a manner? These actions were not planned. They are merely a response. But a response to what? Stress? Evidence will be presented that proves that these responses come from the internal pressures and stresses of the mind." He tapped his right temple with a forefinger and held it there as he stared around the room.

He persisted much more assertively than before. "The accused was suffering such stresses of the mind on that fateful evening. Years of neglect from uncaring and unworthy parents. The victim of bullying from his peers. His general demeanor and will to please others had been used against him. Men and women from every walk of life used him for his meager earnings. He was their fall guy. A simple and uncomplicated man. A just and noble man, pushed beyond the boundaries of his limitations, and we all have limitations." He let the words hang for a while before continuing. "Do you know what yours are?"

He persisted in his current vein of thought. He questioned the concept of always being able to formulate intent before responding. He suggested that we were creatures that always responded on a base level rather than rational human beings capable of rational thought. CC went on to discuss the virtue of hindsight, and at looking at an act with a biased intellectual framework. However, it didn't take long before some members of the jury became restless. Sensing their discomfort, he concluded his opening statement with, "thus, determining the elements of morality and discerning the implications of actions, it is my intention that sufficient doubt will be presented to the court today, and that as a consequence you will find the accused not guilty."

During the last part of the opening statement, he moved around the courtroom expertly. Timing every phrase. Speaking to the jury, and then the public gallery. He even eyed McBean and held the stare until his point was made. He moved across to the prosecution's desk and addressed them. His voice was loud and clear.

He turned to the bench, brought his legs together. His arms were by his side when he bowed. He looked like a tin soldier.

"Thank you, Your Honor."

CHAPTER 53

"Please state your name for the court."

He sat with his back straight, his right leg folded over his left, and his hands in his lap. "Owen Orphelius Restful."

"Profession."

"Psychiatrist, rather a Doctor of Psychiatry."

There were some murmurs around the courtroom. Only some of them had heard the term, yet all of them had no idea what it meant.

"For the benefit of the court, could you please explain the nature of your profession?"

"Most certainly." His voice was crisp, and he came across as self-assured. A real professional, even if he didn't look like it. It was the double shot of brandy he had that morning during breakfast. "Psychiatry is the study of the human mind. The role of the psychiatrist is much like that of a Doctor of Medicine, however, instead of mending broken bones and other such ailments, a psychiatrist identifies the mental processes that cause people to act a certain way and seeks to remedy these either through restructuring thinking processes and or alternative treatments."

"How long have you been a practicing psychiatrist?"

"Approximately twenty years."

"Do you have a private practice?"

"I am currently retired; however, I have previously owned a successful practice."

Cloverfield turned his attention to the bench. "Your Honor, I ask the court to acknowledge Owen Orphelius Restful as an expert witness. I present the doctor's credentials to the court for perusal." He handed McBean the papers, who read through them while the court waited patiently and in silence.

McBean spoke. "Mr. Purcell."

He stood as straight as a telegraph pole. "Your Honor."

"Do you have any objection to the defense request?"

"No objection, Your Honor." He smiled mischievously. It was then that McBean knew that Cloverfield had made an error. The prosecution knew something no one else knew. In fact, McBean believed Purcell was looking forward to the cross-examination.

The judge addressed the witness. "Mr. Restful."

He interrupted the judge. "That's Doctor."

The courtroom cringed. They sensed that correcting the judge in that manner was disrespectful. They were expecting a reprimand and were surprised when it wasn't meted out. McBean considered it, however, took great delight that knowing the cross-examination was going to be painful for Restful and the defense."

McBean smiled condescendingly, "Dr. Restful, from which education facility did you get your degree?"

"Milburn."

"How long did you study psychiatry before you were considered a doctor?"

"Three years." His lip was getting dry.

"Under whose tutelage did you st…" He was rudely cut off.

"Can I have some water?"

The public gallery gasped as one. Surely, he wouldn't let this slight go unaddressed, and they were right.

The esteemed justice has been officiating for years and he had not had the displeasure of questioning such a pompous and arrogant sloth as the man that sat in the witness box. Cloverfield poured him a glass of water and gave him a look that puzzled him.

"Mr. Restful."

"That's Doc…."

His voice was loud and commanding. "Mr. Restful." He paused. The doctor went quiet on the silent urgings of the defense attorney.

"That is three times you have corrected me. The first I put down to nervousness and inexperience in a courtroom. The second and third I put down to arrogance. You will answer my questions. You will not seek correction from me again. If you do, I will find you in contempt of court and throw you in jail. Am I clear?"

The thin veneer of confidence that the early morning brandy and the promise of more to come instilled in him was shattered. He began to shake, and his voice was weak. He looked at the judge meekly. "Yes."

"Yes, Your Honor."

He breathed deeply, uncrossed his legs, and began fidgeting with the buttons of the new suit that had been arranged for him. 'Yes, Your Honor."

"Very well. Before I grant your request, Mr. Cloverfield, I will ask a few more questions of the witness."

"Yes, Your Honor." Cloverfield felt a wash of defeat run right through him. He sat heavily in the chair.

He directed his focus to the man, who in a short period of time he had come to despise. He couldn't wait until Purcell sank his teeth into him. "Under whose tutelage did you study psychiatry at Milburn?"

"Dr. Thinwaller."

"How long has Dr. Thinwaller been a lecturer at Milburn on this topic?"

He scratched his chin, licked his lips, and took another drink of water. "I recollect that he was the lecturer at Milburn for four years before my arrival."

"Have you had your own practice?"

"That's correct, for ten years."

"Was it a successful practice?"

"It was indeed Your Honor." It was a lie but no one else needed to know that.

"Mr. Cloverfield, in light of the credentials presented to the court, and my knowledge of the Milburn academy and with no objection from the prosecution, the court acknowledges Owen Orphelius Restful as an expert witness." He smiled inwardly. He had a strong feeling that Cloverfield had made another mistake.

"Thank you, Your Honor."

"You may continue your questioning."

"Very well." Cloverfield bowed slightly, moved around the defense table, and occupied the space between it and the witness box.

"Dr. Restful, are you familiar with the term insanity?"

"Most certainly."

"In your professional practice, have you dealt with cases of insanity before?"

"Yes, twice as I recall."

"Could you please explain the definition of the term."

He turned to the jury, as they practiced, and said, "the term refers to a temporary or permanent loss of self in which one is unable to distinguish the difference between right and wrong."

"Have you examined the accused?"

"Yes, I have."

"Have you made a determination as to the state of mind of the accused at the time of the unfortunate death of Mr. Jenkins?"

"I have."

"What is this determination?"

"That the accused suffered from a temporary loss of mind at the time of the killing."

"Could you please explain that another way?"

"Of course." He was feeling confident again. He resumed the posture of a confident man and persisted. "In my professional opinion the accused was not in his right mind when he killed the deceased."

"What led you to this conclusion?"

"Years of abuse by his parents, and the mistreatment of others over the years led him to develop a complex range of anxieties. These boiled over the years like water in a kettle, until he was unable to control his emotions and, for want of a better word, he snapped."

"Meaning?"

"That he was unable to control his mind. Therefore, this led to actions which were completely out of character. Unfortunately, these actions resulted in a man's death. A death for which he was not clinically responsible."

"Clinically responsible?"

"That means that he was not of sound mind, which is normal, at the time of the killing."

"That is all Your Honor. The defense requests a recess before cross-examination."

"Request denied. The prosecution may cross-examine."

CHAPTER 54

Purcell addressed the jury, after nodding to the bench and the public gallery. "I will try not to waste much of the court's time." He moved across to stand at the witness box and stared at Restful. "What makes you qualified to testify in this courtroom?"

"Objection."

"Sustained. Need I remind the prosecution that they accepted the witnesses' credentials, and thus agreed that Dr. Restful had the authority to act as an expert witness in this case?"

"I apologize to the court, Your Honor."

"Very well, you may proceed."

"Is psychiatry a reliable field of medicine?"

"Yes, I believe so."

"Can you always determine a person's state of mind?"

There was a pause, a reluctant pause. "It's not as simple as that. Psychiatry is a complex science."

"Can you always determine a person's state of mind?"

"Objection. The question has been asked and answered."

McBean smiled. "The question has been asked; however, it most certainly has not been answered. You may proceed, Mr. Purcell."

"I am reluctant to ask the question a third time in case there is another objection."

The public gallery and many members of the jury grave a wry laugh.

"The prosecution will refrain from making arbitrary comments," ordered McBean.

Purcell ignored the judge. He was tired and lonely. He wanted to go home. There was a lady friend of his he was eager to contact. "Can you always determine a person's state of mind? Yes or no."

"No. It is impossible to always be in a position to do so."

"Excellent. Were you there the night that Mr. Jenkins was murdered?"

"Objection." Cloverfield was flabbergasted. "The court has not decided that a murder occurred."

"This is the second time that the prosecution has used such language. You are walking a thin line; tread carefully."

The prosecutor moved across to the table and whispered to Boggins. They conversed for a moment before Purcell began his line of questioning. He addressed his next question to the judge. "Your Honor, as Dr. Restful is acknowledged by the court as an expert witness. I seek leave to question his credibility as a practitioner, as a business owner and as a man." This was Cloverfield's error. An expert witness may be subject to harsh scrutiny through cross-examination. The validity of his testimony will hinge upon the reputation of the person giving it and this is what Purcell intended to expose.

"Permission granted."

"Objection. The prosecution…" Before he could finish, McBean spoke over the top of him.

"When the defense sought to establish the doctor as an expert witness, they also knew that the credibility of the witness could be questioned. Sit down, Mr. Cloverfield."

Mcbean addressed the court. "I have had enough of these shenanigans. The next person that laughs will be removed. The next legal representative that acts inappropriately will be held in contempt and jailed for thirty days. The next witness that disrespects the courtroom will also face imprisonment." He pounded the gavel once, but it sent a message, and that message was clear. "Continue."

Purcell stood in front of Restful, folded his arms and swayed gently. "When did you arrive in town?"

"Two or three nights ago."

"Did you arrive on the evening stage?"

"Yes."

"Who was there to meet you?"

"Cletus, I mean Mr. Cloverfield."

"Were you drunk when you got off the stage?"

He looked around and took some time to find the right words.

"Need I remind you, that you are under oath?"

Restful tried, oh how he had tried. When he had received a message from the lawyer, a long time ago, he jumped at the chance. Now it was plain to see that once again he had failed. He began to shake, his shoulders slumped, and he looked defeated.

"Objection on the basis of relevance," complained his lawyer.

"That relevance has been established. Carry on, Mr. Purcell."

"Were you drunk when you arrived on the stage?"

His voice was that of a defeated man. "Yes."

"Do you have a problem with alcohol?"

"Yes."

"You were married, is that correct?"

"Yes."

"How did that marriage end?"

"Divorce."

"Did alcohol play a part in the breakdown of the marriage?"

What could he say? He couldn't lie. There was no point lying anymore. "Yes."

"Your practice failed, didn't it?"

"Yes."

"Why?"

"Two reasons. Lack of clients, and I drank too much."

"Have you continued your study since graduating from Milburn?"

"No."

"Have you ever been prevented from testifying before?"

"No." Short answers were always the best.

"Have you written any peer reviewed journals on psychiatry?"

"No."

"Have you conducted independent research in the field of psychiatry?"

"No."

Cloverfield closed his eyes. There was no use objecting. He knew the response. Restful was sinking fast and he and Noble were going down with him.

"Have you worked with other experts since your graduation, I mean for consulting purposes or for any other professional reason?"

"No."

'How many times did you examine the accused?"

"Once."

"Only once?"

"That's right."

"When did you examine the accused?"

"Last night."

"How long did you examine the accused?"

"A little over an hour."

"Let me get this right. By your estimation, you have been in town two or three days and have spoken to the accused for little over an hour, which took place last night."

"Correct."

"If I may, Your Honor, I would like to repeat my opening question. By doing so I mean no disrespect, I am simply trying to understand the credentials of the witness. The prosecution acknowledges that the witness has a degree in psychiatry and that it was obtained lawfully from a legal institution, however, there are serious concerns as to the credibility of the witness."

"You may ask the question." McBean stifled both a yawn and a smile.

Purcell was taking delight in the scene. "Dr. Owen Orphelius Restful, apart from having a degree in psychiatry, what makes you qualified to testify in this courtroom today?"

CHAPTER 55

The decimation of the expert witness was complete. Court was adjourned for closing statements the following day, until then it was business as usual. Joe Denning was sitting in his office filing through some papers, when there was a sharp yet gentle knock on his office door. "Enter."

His secretary Margaret Smee entered. She was an officious if terse woman. Portly and square framed with a round chin and black glasses. Middle-aged and determined. She was an excellent employee, and though he had given clear instructions not to be disturbed, if she did so it was for a good reason. "A Mr. Festus Rasmussen is here to see you. He says it is about the sale of some mines."

He became quite animated and began stacking papers and placing them on the edge of the desk. "Please send Mr. Rasmussen in, hurry along now."

Thirty seconds later Festus Rasmussen entered, and the secretary closed the door behind him. Denning stood and greeted the man like he was a long-lost friend. They shook hands and Denning indicated for the visitor to sit.

"So good to see you, Mr. Rasmussen," he spoke fast. "I'm sorry to hear about your partners. First Jake and then Deadeye. Yes sir, an unfortunate series of events. Must take a toll on a man, losing his best friends in such a short time and in such a violent manner."

Festus shrugged. He was out of his depth, and he couldn't hold a decent conversation with anyone in a social class higher than himself. He just didn't have the faculties to engage in the same way. He figured it was the environment that threw him off kilter. On the other hand, if they were at the Western Palace then it would be a different game altogether. He simply removed a folded piece of paper and handed it to Denning and waited for a reply.

"I could offer you five thousand less. I am afraid that it's the best I can do."

He expected the negotiation to go this way. He was polite, but abrupt. "No deal."

Denning figured the lunkhead would be a pushover. Little did he know that he was pigheaded when he needed to be, especially when he was instructed to do so. "Times are tough sir and I imagine that you would be feeling the pinch as well. I could go no less than three thousand below your requested price, and that is my bottom line."

Festus reached across and gently removed the paper from Dennings's hand, folded it and put it back in his pocket. "I am sorry we couldn't agree on a price." He stood and moved to the door. He was halfway through the reception area when the banker/lawyer caught up to him and ushered him back into his office. "There's no need to be hasty, Mr. Rasmussen. I am sure we can work something out." He closed the door behind them and urged the big man to sit.

It was the lunkhead's turn to up the ante. "My price is firm, Mr. Denning. I will not accept a cent less. You've been after the property for years. Every time you saw Deadeye in town you made an offer. You were right to consider him the brains of the outfit, but he told me what the mines were worth, and I trust him. I am moving on with my life sir. There's nothing here for me anymore. Going to head west to Santa Fe, find me a senorita and have some fun for a change. I am tired sir. Tired of hard work. Tired of slaving away. I'm tired sweating from toil. I'm worn out. A man must have some leisure in his life. Don't you think so, Mr. Denning?"

He was only paying mild attention to the big man. It was true that he had been after the mines for a few years now, he just didn't figure on paying top dollar. "Is anyone else interested in the property?"

"I haven't asked around, but there's always someone willing to pay a price for the chance at a jackpot. Jake, Deadeye, and I did, and we found some dust that kept us going. It's a hard life sir, but a man could invest, and a mighty fine investment it is too. Deadeye also taught me that."

"You miss him, don't you?"

"More than a man is likely to miss another man. He was like kin to me."

"He was an interesting character."

"He was my best friend."

Denning leaned on the desk. Though he was a lawyer, he had never set a day in a courtroom as a practicing attorney. He preferred conveyancing and contract law, but he only indulged in this profession as a favor, as he was also in the business of banking favors as well.

"I'll tell you what I will do." He made it sound like he was doing Rasmussen a favor. "I'll pay the price you demand if you leave all the equipment behind. That includes picks, shovels, sifting pans, cups, and plates. I mean everything."

Festus had no plans of returning. "Deal." They shook hands.

"I will draw up the papers myself. Give me a couple of days and we will settle."

He removed another piece of folded paper and handed it to Denning. "I'm leaving in the morning. Put the money in this account. I'll sign the papers before I leave, and I will draw a hundred dollars in cash for my travels." He stood and moved to the door. "I understand that you've got jury service, so please make the necessary arrangements."

Denning wasn't expecting such a hasty departure, but for the sake of the property he would act swiftly. "Are you not staying to hear the verdict?" This was a reasonable question considering the circumstances.

"Jenkins was your partner."

"Indeed, he was. God will deliver justice. All sinners meet a gruesome fate. It's called hell. Reverend Blair taught me that."

"The papers will be ready for you to sign. I'll leave them with Miss. Smee, along with the cash and a receipt for the balance in the nominated account."

"Thanks, Joe."

Before the banker could move around the desk and shake his hand goodbye, Rasmussen marched across the main room and exited through the front door.

CHAPTER 56

Hammond's funeral was a solemn affair. Only a handful of people had time to make their presence known. Reverend Blair was more solemn and more forgiving than previously. This was simply because the crowd was so small. The greater the crowd the more he rose to the occasion. Ernest grumbled when the service finished. He had to finish digging another hole for Johns and fill one in. He complained to the wind, for the labor had taken a toll on his old body. He should give the game away like Walter, and just like Walter, he should find a woman to dote over.

Walter and Merle Overall had become inseparable. They spent every minute from dawn to dusk together. They kept polite company and spent this mostly in the garden of her delightful home or by the fire. They would recount stories of their youth, in a wholesome and just manner. The dances they had attended, the parties and events held by the town council, but these events were infrequent now. There was less community than there had been back in their childhood. They rued lost opportunities, but most of all they found solace and comfort in one another. Though they had always been cordial to one another their close companionship has a feeling of permanence. This evening, they were sitting by the fire. Walter was reading, for despite his age his eyes were perfect, and next to him Merle was rocking in her chair knitting. He never stayed over of course, as that would be scandalous, but there was time yet to sit in silence and let the world pass by. That's exactly what they did. Walter had been the telegrapher since its invention. Prior to that, as a young man he traveled a little and tried his hand at most jobs. Together they had decided that the world changes because people change. For better or for worse there was no use complaining.

Back at the jailhouse Millie Tippet spoke with her enamored bad boy, Timothy Noble. Their conversations were more relaxed, and there was less emphasis on the bible, and life hereafter. They had allowed hope to entertain them. Hope that he will be cleared of the charges. If not cleared, then perhaps a few years in jail. She could wait. She would wait. They would marry, and even start a family of their own. It was obvious to her that he was remorseful. He prayed for forgiveness every day. The irony is that not once did he pray for the man he killed and for his family. Wrongdoers seek forgiveness from their sins to absolve their conscience from a life of turmoil. Still their time together was genuine, and Wells has permitted the visits to run overtime. The quieter they were the longer they spent together.

Her voice was soft and delicate. "Are you sure you're making the right decision?"

Noble shrugged his shoulders. "I have nothing to lose."

"What about a plea bargain? You could get some time in jail. I will wait, you know that. At least you will be alive."

"According to Cloverfield, he has requested such a negotiation with Purcell, but he was refused."
"Why?"
He choked on his words, "because Purcell senses victory, and I expect a hanging would be more expedient for his political career. At least that's what my lawyer said."

"Once you say it like that, I suppose you have no choice but to testify."

She reached through the cell door and held his hands. They prayed silently together, and before time was up Millie made a vow to stand by his side no matter what happened.

Cloverfield was drunk again. The first drink was to take the edge off the series of events that unfolded in the courtroom earlier that day. Then he drank to drown his sorrows. The drunker he got the angrier he got. He wasn't mad at the prosecutor, Purcell, nor McBean. He had given up on Restful as being a hopeless drunk and a fool. The person he was most angry at was himself. He had let his client down and now he had no option but to put Noble on the stand. He was terrified of the prospect, as Purcell would be out for blood. He had given Noble the option and he jumped at the chance to tell his side of the story. There is always hope and, just maybe he could sway one jury member to feel compassion for his plight.

Cloverfield realized that he had imbibed in too many beverages and his closing statement was poetic and arbitrary. It appealed to the emotions of the jury members, not the cold hard facts of the case. Facts. What use were facts? There was no place for truth in the legal system. It was all about who had the best argument, and at this stage it was the prosecution.

CHAPTER 57

Judge McBean was feeling poorly; thus, the court resumed a little after lunch. During the morning Denning was on hand to go through the legal papers with Rasmussen, who was content with the arrangement. They shook hands and parted. The former miner's next stop was the store, where he spent some time talking to Ned and gathering some supplies for a long trip. To Santa Fe he said. Ned had once been to Santa Fe and took great delight in telling Festus all about it. Once he was loaded and prepared for departure, he hitched out front of the sheriff's office. It was an unusual visit, and to protect Noble, Sheriff Wells stepped into the daylight on a crooked foot to meet the visitor.

"Good morning, Festus. Headed somewhere?" He pointed to his well-stocked, and well-fed bay.

"Leaving town, Sheriff. I just wanted to make sure that I was good to leave. I'm planning on living a leisurely life and I don't want any warrant out for my arrest."

He was referring to being questioned over the rock throwing incident. "The law needs evidence Festus. It has none, you are free to go."

"Thanks, Sheriff."

"For what it's worth, I don't think it was you who threw the rock."

"Much obliged for that, Sheriff. I hate being blamed for something I didn't do."

"Where are you headed?"

"Santa Fe."

"That's a long way from here."

"Just what I need."

"What about the mines?"

"Sold to Denning. I recall Deadeye and Jake talking about how he always pestered them to sell. I thought it was the right move. There's nothing for me in Rocksprings anymore."

"Isn't it strange how life works out?"

"Sure is, Sheriff."

"Not hanging around to see the outcome of the trial."

He shook his head. "I'm not a genius, Sheriff, but I figure he'll be found guilty, and hang. I have no doubt about that. I can live with knowing that all the same." He produced another folded piece of paper and handed it to the lawman.

"What's this?"

"Fancy writing isn't it. I asked Joe to write it for me. It's my sister's address in Santa Fe. I would appreciate it if you could send me word about the trial."

"The trial will finish any day now. You could hang around, even watch the hanging if that's how it plays out."

He shook his head. "I've got the itch, Sheriff, and I've got to scratch it."

Wells placed the paper in his pocket. "Sure thing, Festus. I'll send you word."

"Thanks, I guess I won't be seeing you, but I sure appreciate it."

They shook hands.

Wells watched the man mount, ride down the long main street and head west toward Santa Fe. He crossed the street, and went to the store, but it was closed. He missed the previous day in court, and he was glad he did. He didn't think he could stomach the humiliation of the expert witness, but now Noble was to testify. This could get ugly. Duty compelled him onward. He returned to the office and Poole was waiting for him, while Swan was at the courthouse ensuring the crowd moved into the room and settled in a prompt manner. They were the instructions from McBean, and Swan was keen to impress. Thirty minutes later Noble was brought through the back door of the building. The people of Rocksprings were waiting in anticipation for the rumor that had spread that the man, the accused, who had not said a word in court was about to tell his side of the story.

CHAPTER 58

You could hear a pin drop. Such was the tension in the courtroom. Boggins, the spy who watched Restful get off the stage, sat shuffling papers. Purcell sat with his arms folded. He looked bored. He had conducted himself honorably throughout the trial. He was confident and deservedly so. He had been notified that Noble would testify in his defense. He was like a hungry dog and Noble was the prey. The prosecution couldn't wait to sink their teeth into the fresh kill. On the other hand, the defense attorney was clear-headed, despite the consumption of alcohol the night before. Focus on the facts, Cletus. He kept telling himself. He had spent so much time dancing around the issues. It was time to focus on the truth. Facts. Facts. Facts. He had tried to be too clever. Noble had been too much in love with Miss. Tippet to notice many of the mistakes he made. From the start everyone considered that it was an impossible case to win. It was in fact, difficult but in his experience nothing was impossible. The credibility of Restful had been refuted, and as a result he did not have many cards left to play. Hence why Noble was to be called to the stand. In his time with Noble he had come to believe that he was a simple man, slow-fitted and at times dull. He believed wholeheartedly that the man had suffered from years of torment, and that he had snapped, and lost control. He just needed one member of the jury to believe the same.

"All rise." The clerk's voice was crisp.

Everyone stood, while the judge shuffled in on a wooden cane. He looked pale, and weary. He looked around the room and paused before sitting.

"Be seated."

McBean's voice was raspy. He spoke to the court. "Today we will hear the testimony of the accused, along with the cross-examination. The defense will close its case. The prosecution and defense will deliver their closing statement tomorrow morning and then the jury will enter deliberation. I expect a verdict sometime tomorrow afternoon or on the morning of the following day." He cleared his throat. "The defense may call its next witness."

Cloverfield stood. "The defense calls Timothy Noble to the stand."

After a minute of shuffling to the witness box in chains he was ready to proceed.

"Please state your name for the court."

"Timothy Noble."

"Where were you born?"

"Littlefield, a small place near Lubbock."

"Did you live in town?"

"A few miles out of town."

"Who was your father?"

"William McMasters Noble." His voice was childlike and high.

"What did your father do for a profession?"

"He had many, so called professions."

"Can you please elaborate?"

"Well, he was a preacher, a horse thief and a bootlegger."

"A dishonest preacher. Heaven forbids."

This drew some wry laughter from the courtroom. Even McBean managed a smile.

The lawyer reminded himself to keep it simple. Don't try to get too elaborate and focus on the facts. "Was he a good father?"

"He was mean, a thug and a hypocrite. So, no, he was not a good father."

"In what way was he mean?"

"He would beat me for the slightest infringement. For example, if I forgot to feed the goats, or if I didn't wash the dishes clean enough."

"How would he beat you?"

"With a belt mostly, that is until I got too big, and he became too drunk to care. From that moment on I was left to fend for myself."

"At what age did he stop, as you said, to care?"

"Not long after my mother died, so about twelve."

"Please, tell the court about your mother."

"Her name was Mary Ann."

"What was she like?"

"Mean, and cold. Distant and uncaring."

"How did she treat you?"

"Poorly. I was homeschooled. I was isolated from other children. I rarely got to speak to people my age."

"Can you give the court an example of how she treated you poorly?"

"Well, as I said, I was homeschooled, and she used to beat me with the ruler if I didn't learn properly."

Millie Tippet, who had heard all this before, dabbed her eyes with a silk handkerchief to dry the tears. Her breast was heaving in sadness. The rest of the public gallery were intrigued. It was a nice story, a little sad, yet in many ways not much different to how they were raised. While they could empathize with the accused, they had difficulty in accepting his upbringing as a justification for murder.

"You said before that your mother was cold. Could you explain what you mean by that?"

"Unloving. I mean both of my parents were drunks. Even when my father remarried, he married a drunk."

"What was your stepmother's name?"

"Margaret Fontaine."

"What type of woman was she?"

"She didn't care for me. I had to cook my own dinner, wash my clothes, and tend to the chores. My education ceased when my mother died."

"How did your father and stepmother die?"

"They were murdered. Their bullet ridden bodies were found out front of the barn in which they operated their bootlegging business. The barn was on fire."

"Did they find the people responsible for their murder?"

"No, though they did suspect it was a rival of my father's business interests."

"What did you do after your parents were murdered?"

"I sold the house, put the money in the bank and left Littlefield behind?"

"Why?"

"Too many bad memories. I couldn't live at that place. I feared I would be next."

"What do you mean, next?"

"Murdered."

Cloverfield paused. He was feeling good, though he had anticipated several objections from Purcell who was waiting patiently. Once again, he reminded himself to stick to the facts.

"Where did you go?"

"I wandered around for a while, until I ended up at a place called Telegraph."

"Tell me about your time in Telegraph."

"I met some nice people, and it wasn't long before I settled in. It wasn't until I met Jasper that I started to realize that those I thought were my friends were using me for what money I had left."

"Can you give an example?"

"I would buy alcohol, and tobacco for my friends or I would settle debts to avoid a violent confrontation. Jasper was a real friend. He didn't ask for money. He didn't drink. He loved fishing."

"What happened to Jasper?"

"He drowned."

"Did you make any more real friends like Jasper in Telegraph?"

He nodded his head and wiped a tear from his eye. Millie sobbed. "Delores."

"What was your relationship with Delores?"

"We were engaged to be married?"

"You were engaged, what happened?"

"She was murdered."

"How?"

He cried some more, and it was obvious that the man was hurting. "Her throat was cut?"

"Did they find her killer?"

"I'm not sure. We, the preacher, and I, buried her by the river and I left Telegraph the following day."

"Where did you go then?"

"Here, I wish I hadn't, but I came to Rocksprings."

"And the incident with Mr. Jenkins, when did that take place?"

"No more than an hour after I arrived in town."

"Why did you go to the Western Palace?"

"Company. I like company. I was starved of it as a child. I feel safer when people are around me."

"Were you seeking any particular kind of comfort?"

"Yes sir, I was seeking the comfort of a whore."

All eyes went to Doris, who sat in the first row of the gallery.

Millie blushed a little. Of course, her admirer had told her everything. Honesty and the lord were at the basis of their relationship.

"What happened?"

"I was approached by her." He pointed to Doris, and once again all eyes except those of Miss. Tippet found her. Doris carried herself with dignity. It wasn't the first time her reputation had been impugned by her profession.

"And then." He was nudged gently by his lawyer to expand.

"I changed my mind and rejected her advances."

"Why?"

"Honestly?"

"We are in a court of law. Honesty is essential."

There was more wry laughter, but it settled quickly.

"She smelled of sweat. It made me change my mind. I left the palace. I was not in there longer than ten minutes."

"You must have been surprised when you were accosted by the deceased."

"Yes sir."

"And confused."

"Objection. That is the second time that counsel has led the witness."

"Sustained. Ask the question, do not assume the accused state of mind."

"Of course, Your Honor. I apologize."

"How did you feel?"

"Surprised and confused."

More laughter, but once again it settled quickly.

"What was Mr. Jenkins' demeanor?"

"He was aggressive. He wouldn't let me leave?"

"What happened?"

"He hit me. I didn't fight back. He held my head underwater and then the next thing I know is that it was morning."

"You remember nothing else."

"That's right sir. Not a thing."

"Do you remember punching the deceased?"

"No."

"Do you recall being yelled at to stop?"

"No."

"Has this ever happened to you before?"

"No."

"Why do you think this is?"

"Objection, Your Honor. The accused is not qualified to give a medical diagnosis."

"Sustained."

Cloverfield was out of ideas. He had nothing left. "No more questions, Your Honor."

"Excellent," muttered McBean. The prosecution may cross-examine.

To the surprise of the court, it was Boggins that stood and addressed the witness. He was a short man, balding with rimmed glasses. It was these he took off and wiped on his tie as he moved across the floor.

"If your parents were so bad, why did you stay with them until you were twenty?"

"Excuse me?"

"You were a grown man at this stage, and you could make decisions. Is that right?"

"Yes well, I, well I don't know why I didn't leave earlier."

"When did your father stop mistreating you?"

"Not long after mother passed."

"So, you said this was when you were about twelve?"

"That is correct."

"What was your life like from the age of twelve to the time you sold the property and moved on?"

"Bearable."

"Were you mistreated during this time?"

"No."

"At the age of twenty you sold the house, banked the proceeds of the sale, and left. These are rational decisions. Would you agree?"

"Please explain."

"The word rational means well thought and logical. In other words, you knew what you were doing."

"I suppose so."

"How did you meet your fiancé, Delores?"

"He choked on the words. "I was a customer."

"Are you saying she was a prostitute?"

"I am."

"How long did you know Delores before you became engaged?"

"Three to four months."

"Did she continue to whore after becoming engaged?"

He nodded. "Yes."

"Did that make you angry?"

"It was her choice. I respected that."

"Did you get angry when she was murdered?"

"I think so, I was mostly upset."

"Your fiancé was murdered, and you think you got angry. When your friend died, did you get angry?"

"I don't believe so."

"Do you get angry often?"

"No, not really."

"Objection." Cloverfield needed to object. He had no real grounds, but he needed to ensure his client some time to regather his thoughts. "Relevance of this particular line of questioning."

Boggins was smug and walked with a swagger. "Your Honor, the relevance of whether the accused is quick or prone to anger is essential in establishing his state of mind, not only on that fateful night, but it all allows the court to distinguish between his capacity to anger and the loss of mind, which is at the heart of the defense. The prosecution must be able to challenge this crucial evidence, therefore his tendency to anger is relevant to the case. For it is the prosecution's intention that the accused did not suffer from a loss of mind, rather became angry, and that it is this anger that caused him to bludgeon the deceased to death."

McBean listened intently. The prosecution was right, but he held the courtroom for a moment before responding. "The line of questioning is relevant. The prosecution may continue."

It was at this time that Boggins dropped a bombshell. "Your Honor, I would like to admit into evidence a signed affidavit by Deputies Thomas Swan and Wilson Poole in which the defendant threatened to kill Deputy Swan."

"Objection. The defense has not been given prior notice of the evidence now tended to the court."

There was a general uproar, and after a few pounds of the gavel the room fell silent. The proceedings were just too interesting to miss.

"Has this evidence been presented to the defense for examination?"

"Yes, Your Honor."

"Judge," the under-pressure lawyer responded, "I have not received a copy of the affidavit."

Boggins pushed. "It is my information that the clerk presented counsel with the required paperwork a number of days ago."

The clerk who made copies of all paperwork as reference for the court was motioned to the bench where a private conversation took place. Meanwhile Cloverfield searched his papers in front of him, and hesitated when he found the affidavit. How had he missed it? Pure incompetence. That's what it was, pure incompetence. His world began spinning, he gulped dry air, and felt sick.

"Your Honor," he stuttered as he held onto the edge of the desk to prevent himself from falling, "I recall receiving the paperwork, and am familiar with the allegations."

The room went silent. Boggins and Purcell looked at one another, and the latter winked and smiled. McBean watched Cloverfield and the clerk sit down. After an awkward moment there was no need for anyone to speak so the accused did all the talking.

Noble stood, his voice became louder, and he pointed his finger at Boggins. "That's right. I threatened him. I told him I'd kill him if he laid a hand on her."

Boggins had to raise his voice. "Laid hands on who?"

Noble sat down and shook his head without saying a word. Boggins sensed an opportunity and the man marched across the room in a confrontational manner and leaned on the witness box. "Who?"

"Me." An unbelievable scene unfolded as Millie Tippet stood in the public gallery. People began pointing and whispering. It was now a public scandal. McBean pounded his gavel and raised his voice. "Deputy Poole, remove that woman from the courtroom."

Miss. Tippet obliged and exited before Poole could get to her. McBean continued to pound his gavel. He raised his voice. "The cross-examination will continue. The next person who speaks will be removed."

Boggins smirked at Noble and turned to the judge. "That's all, Your Honor."

"Mr. Cloverfield, do you have any more witnesses?"

It was the voice and movements of a defeated man. His face was ashen gray. He looked sickly pale. "The defense rests."

"For a moment there, I thought I was in a real courtroom, where people conducted themselves with the dignity and respect that such a case of this stature deserves. Instead, we have this. Closing statements will be at nine o'clock tomorrow morning. Dismissed."

"All rise."

McBean exited decidedly faster than when he entered and slammed the door closed behind him.

CHAPTER 59

Festus Rasmussen rode a well-rested bay northeast out of Rocksprings toward New Mexico. A mile out of town he veered northeast and took a back trail to Telegraph. He knew the area well. He, Deadeye and Jenkins, when they weren't working in the mines, which was quite often, scoured the countryside within two days' ride of town for stray beef, or anything else they could purloin. Of course, they were suspected of petty theft, but there were no witnesses and no evidence. The trio were rough around the edges, and were judged merely by their appearance, which was disheveled and uncleansed. They didn't fit into the normal conventions of civil life. Society, whatever that meant, didn't accept them, not that they tried to fit in. They did not wish to live outside of the social dimension of Rocksprings. Society offered them many benefits, most importantly protection from the law. Still, they roamed aimless and free as they could in a world that had no time or place for them. Whether that was true or not it didn't matter. Perception shapes reality, and the isolation they felt and experienced was a reality for many men after the war.

He rode thirty miles on the first day, riding well into the night until he reached Telegraph. His entrance to the small place, especially at that time of night, went unnoticed. He slept in a cold camp a mile north of the town, before rising a little after sunrise, and continuing his journey east. Resting around mid-morning in a clump of cottonwood, he fed the bay some grain and gave the horse its head and let it drink from a silty creek nearby. He ate some hardtack and swallowed this down with some water from a dirty canteen. This was quickly followed by a hefty swig of brandy which after some deliberation, he recorked and stowed away.

Reverend Blair had gotten inside his head. Talk of sin, eternity and burning in the fires of hell plagued his thoughts. If the reverend was right then he was in for a hell of time, that is unless he repented. To repent he would have to acknowledge his wrongs, give his life to God, and commit to living a righteous life. On the surface it seemed so easy, but habits were hard to break.

A coyote watched him from a rock. By the time he removed his Winchester from the scabbard the coyote sensed danger and disappeared. They were skittish creatures. Prone to secrecy and deception. He was a coyote. Thievery. Lying. Murder. Lust. Sin. He committed them all. There was a time in prison that he had killed just to make a statement. Statements were needed and a man, in his own way, needed to make his own. He needed to draw a line in the sand. He bashed in the brains of an impending rival with a rock. The message was clear, leave me and mine alone.

He sweated profusely and it wasn't long before he rested again. It was a little after midday and he had reached his destination. It was just as he had described. It was a desert oasis. A semicircle of cottonwood crested a pool of clear, clean, and cool water. Dismounting he unpacked the bay and removed the saddle. He picketed the mount with a long lead. There was plenty of ground cover to keep the horse busy for a while. He laid his blanket on the earth in the shade and stripped off all his clothes before having the first bath he had in a long time.

He collected firewood which was plentiful and dry. There was plenty of daylight, so he laid down and closed his eyes. He fell asleep instantly, however instead of sweet dreams, he tossed and turned in a feverish sweat. He dreamed that he was in hell, flames flickered all around him. He could hear Jenkins and Deadeye call out for him, but he was lost in the furnace. He could hear people screaming in agony. He watched as Reverend Blair took it upon himself to lecture the devil on the virtues of humility and grace. When was the last time he was humble? When was the last time he was graceful? It wasn't very graceful of him to lie to Sheriff Wells about going to his sisters in Santa Fe. He didn't have a sister. Nor was it right to lie to Denning, or Doris. What about Tina Evergreen? Nor was it right to mislead the reverend. He woke in a heavy sweat. Overcome with guilt and confusion he uncorked the bottle of brandy and drank heartily. It was at about this time that the jury had been given their instructions from the tired, fed up and cantankerous old sod, Judge McBean.

CHAPTER 60

The jury of twelve men retired to a designated room in the courthouse to deliberate. A man by the name of Cyril Green, a prosperous entrepreneur in the cattle industry was elected the foreman of the jury. It was a task he took seriously. Sitting at the head of the long table, he eyed the jurors speculatively. They were from the upper echelons of polite society and included Joe Denning and Ned the store owner. Other members included Xavier Burns, a part-time dentist. Harold Fitzburg, the owner of the stage, and Heath Durban, the proprietor of the Cutting D Ranch. "What happens now?" muttered the only member of the jury that didn't run in the same circles of the others. His name was James Fallon. It was a fair question and one they have all considered, which all but one was afraid to ask. Green dominated the proceedings.

"Fair question, James." We will go around the room and say whether the defendant is guilty or not guilty and then we can take it from there."

They nodded and mumbled their consent in unison.

"I'll go first. I say that the accused is guilty."

"Joe."

"Guilty."

"Ned."

"Guilty."

And so, it went. Each juror in turn declared the accused, Timothy Noble, was guilty.

"Now what?" Asked Ned.

"Seems to me," said James Fallon, "that each of us ought to be able to state why we find him guilty of murder."

"Very good, James," responded Green. Though truth be told he was annoyed at not having produced the idea himself. "Would you like to start, James."

"Sure. There was simply no evidence presented by the defense that cast doubt on the actions of the accused. Besides that, the prosecution provided ample evidence to indicate that the murder was carried out by the accused, a fact which the defense agrees with."

"But does he intend to kill him? That's the part I am stuck on." The man who spoke was Kent Verrills. Another local member of the Chamber of Commerce. He continued, "at that moment, when did he make the conscious decision to kill?" Before the other could offer their injections, he held up his hands indicating to them that he hadn't finished. "I think he did. He grabbed Jenkins, who was unconscious at the time, by the hair and persisted in punching him. To me that proves intent."

It was a valid statement, and hard to counter.

The men began discussing the case amongst them themselves and examining the evidence as it was laid out in court. They all believed the man was guilty, but they needed to be able to articulate why.

The foreman of the jury requested a pencil and paper. Once received he interrupted their chatter. "Let's walk through the facts of the act as we know them to be, and then let's decide. Remember that there must be no doubt. They nodded in agreement. Too bad if they didn't because Green, who considered himself important in Rocksprings, began.

"Jenkins and the accused had a confrontation on the night in question."

"That's correct. Yes." The rest nodded.

"The confrontation was because of the accused knocking over Miss. Ahoy," he used the moniker sheepishly, "and refused to apologize."

They signaled their agreement, and he continued.

"A fracas ensued. The accused claimed that he tried to walk away, conflicts with witness testimony that he stepped aggressively toward Jenkins."

"Enraged, the accused knocked the deceased unconscious, straddled him, grabbed him by the hair and continued to punch him. That is despite being yelled at to stop and shrugging off the blacksmith, Fotheringham, who was doing his civic duty by trying to stop the outrage. The accused continued his attack until Sheriff Wells brought an end to it by bringing the barrel of his shotgun down across his head and knocking him unconscious." He took a breath. "Are those the facts of the case as we know them to be?"

"That's correct. Yes." The rest nodded. There was nothing else to be said.

Sensing he had their attention, he persisted. "There was no evidence presented to the court about the accused's allegations of mistreatment from his parents.

Or of being bullied, and by whom. It was mere speculation. Dr. Restful," they all giggled, "decided on his client's state of mind, after a one-hour consultation. Which was conducted approximately five weeks after the event. He provided no evidence to substantiate the claims of insanity at the time of Mr. Jenkins death."

"Are we in agreement?"

They all nodded.

"Excellent. I will start and we will go back around the room, and we will all give our verdict based on the facts of the case. I say that the accused is guilty of murder."

"Joe."

"Guilty of murder." He followed Cyril Green's lead on using the appropriate terminology.

So did Ned. "Guilty of murder."

And so, it went. Each juror in turn declared the accused, Timothy Noble, was guilty of murder.

CHAPTER 61

The accused Timothy Noble and his lawyer sat in the small room at the back of the courthouse. It was a space the accused had become familiar with over the last week. He was pacing back and forth on one side of the small room, while his lawyer sat with his head in his hands. It was Noble who broke the silence.

"I should not have lost my temper."

Cloverfield raised his weary head. "Yeah, well we have all made mistakes."

Noble patted his lawyer on the shoulder. "We were never going to win this case. Even if Dr. Restful had been useful. A town like this won't let a stranger walk free. Not after this."

CC tried to be positive. "They haven't found you guilty yet. I know it's difficult, but you must try and remain positive."

He paced back and forth some more. "Do you have a pencil and paper?"

The lawyer fumbled in his briefcase and handed them over. "What are you doing?"

"I am writing my will, and I expect you to witness it."

For ten minutes the only sound in that small room was the scribbling of lead on paper. Noble had resigned himself to his impending fate, while Cloverfield was planning his departure. He would leave on the stage that left for Austin. From there he would make the necessary arrangements to head to the east coast. He needed to get as far away from Rocksprings as he could. Yet no matter how far he traveled he needed to reconcile with himself over his incompetence.

His thoughts were interrupted. "Please read and sign."

It took him a few minutes to read it. He signed and folded the paper and put it in his case.

"I have already identified the grounds for appeal. Your fate is far from sealed."

Noble ignored the last-ditch attempt to remain positive. "Will I face the hangman's noose or be sent to jail?"

"Jails are overcrowded; besides I expect them to make an example of you."

"Why?"

"To deter others from performing other such heinous acts."

"Does it work, I mean does hanging people deter others from committing murders?"

"No."

"Then why do they do it?"

"They lean on their morals, sell a message to the people, but the only ones who are buying, are those who don't need to. It helps them, the lousy, shifty, no-good politicians buy votes. There's nothing like being tougher on crime than your opponent."

Purcell and Boggins were sitting on the bench under the tree out front of the courthouse. They were pleased with how the trial played out. There was no doubt in their minds that Noble would be found guilty of murder and sentenced to hang. Upon their arrival to Austin, they would receive a hero's welcome, and a hearty pat on the back from those that mattered.

"You performed excellently, Wilfred. Rest assured that I will spread the word of your prowess in the courtroom."

"Thank you, sir. I will let the governor know, through my sister, of your political qualities. You're just what politics in this country needs."

Purcell smirked, "what, another lawyer?"

Wilfred Boggin's sister was close to the son of the governor. It was a tight arrangement. Those of the same social class gathered in the same private and public spaces. They reinforced their position within society. It was a circle of ambition, intrigue, controversy, and lust yet they all had the same purpose. The expansion of status through the acquisition of power and wealth.

McBean waited alone in his chambers for the verdict. It was a loathsome trial. A tiresome and bothersome debacle as far as he was concerned. This would be his last. He was writing a letter of resignation from the bar. The thought of sitting through another trial made him feel sick. They don't make lawyers like they used to. There was a time, he thought to himself and then he stopped. There was no point reflecting on what was because what was gave birth to what is. If what is, is not great, it is because of what was. Therefore, what was, was clearly not as romantic and ideal as one imagined. He got lost in the thought and poured another whiskey. He was tilting the beverage to his lips when he received a knock on the door.

His voice was weary, "enter."

It was the clerk of the court. "They have reached a verdict Your Honor."

He removed the fob watch from his pocket. "Thank you, we will resume at three o'clock."

It has taken the jury fifty-three minutes to reach a verdict. It was longer than he expected.

Meanwhile, some members of the public milled around the front of the courthouse while the rest waddled down to the Palace to indulge in drink and gossip. There was much happening in Rocksprings and lots to talk about. The murders of Hammond and Johns. The shootout between the law and Thomas Bland who was eventually shot down in the street. The trial. The arrival and departure of Festus Rasmussen with the body of his friend, Deadeye Dave folded across a mule. And Rasmussen's subsequent departure. So, when word came through that the jury had reached a verdict the patrons of the Palace skulled their drinks and made their way back to the courthouse. Whatever would they do for entertainment once the trial was over?

CHAPTER 62

The jury filed into the courtroom from the room beyond, one by one, led by the foreman Cyril Green. Their stern and serious expression gave nothing away. There was some rustling of papers, and then silence. It was McBean's turn to speak.

"Will the accused please stand?"

Noble was sitting at the desk with his lawyer, and they stood together. The latter reached out his arm and patted the defendant on the back and stood with his hands clasped behind him, his head down. He was dreading the verdict. The defendant made the sign of the father, the son, and the holy ghost. He held a bible in his hands and stared at the foreman of the jury.

There were two taps of the gavel that echoed in the room. "Has the jury reached a verdict?"

Cyril Green's voice displayed his confident nature. "It has, Your Honor."

"Very well." McBean cleared his throat. "In the case of the state of Texas versus Timothy Noble for the murder of Jake Jenkins, how do you find the accused?"

His voice was strong, though perhaps unnecessarily loud and determined. "We, the jury, find Timothy Noble guilty of murder."

The verdict was no surprise, still there was a smattering of talk which quickly settled before McBean could reach his gavel.

Purcell and Boggins shook hands.

The defense counsel spoke. "Your Honor, the defense seeks leave to appeal the verdict."

"You may do as you see fit, Mr. Cloverfield. However, you will do it through the proper channels and follow the correct procedure. Is that understood?"

"Yes, Your Honor."

The judge now commanded the room. "It is the duty and responsibility of this court to pass a sentence and in doing so I speak directly to Timothy Noble. Sir, you have been found guilty of murder by a jury of your peers. The manner of the death of the deceased was both vicious and vile. Such an act cannot be tolerated, and the punishment must fit the crime. Therefore, it is my duty to sentence you to hang."

Millie wept into her silk handkerchief, while the rest of the court remained silent.

"You are to be escorted to the Goodwill Penitentiary, where at the governor's convenience you are to be hanged from the neck until you are dead. The law must be morally superior to those that seek to gain advantage from breaking the law. Though you will be shown no mercy, the law demands, and society expects, that you will be treated fairly until such time that your life is forfeited. You will have time to say your goodbyes to your loved ones, an advantage that wasn't afforded to the deceased. You have time to make amends with your deeds and prepare your speech for your maker. This same right was not afforded to the man you murdered. Only those men who can forgive themselves seek forgiveness from others. Until then, pray, live well. Be kind and repent. Repentance without conviction is blasphemous. Repentance without love and compassion is heresy. I see that you grasp tightly to the good book, Mr. Noble. I would like to remind you of Isaiah chapter 1, verse 18 *"Come now, let us settle the matter," says the Lord. "Though your sins are like scarlet, they shall be as white as snow; though they are red as crimson, they shall be like wool."*

He paused, and for the last time looked around the courtroom. The legal system had come to represent everything a young, ambitious, and righteous mind fights against. Corruption and politics. Buffoonery, and deceit. An emotionless and uncaring system that occasionally delivered justice. He shook his head in disgust, as he tasted bile in his throat. It was bitter.

"Case closed."

CHAPTER 63

Noble was shackled by the ankles and his hands were likewise constrained behind his back. Sheriff Wells stood behind him with his shotgun, while Deputy Poole walked ten paces in front of the prisoner. Deputy Swan walked between the prisoner and the side of the street in which the Palace was on. Throughout the trial they had followed the same procedure. Each day, at least an hour after court dispersed the prisoner would be moved. The routine was the same. The lawmen had been on high alert throughout the trial, and no one had even verbally abused the prisoner let alone tried to get to him.

Poole opened the door of the courthouse and looked to his left and right. Swan was next to step into the sunlight. The sun was always high and bright at this time of day, and they looked straight into it. Noble stepped through the door, and as per routine waited while the sheriff closed the door behind him and checked the shackles.

Millie Tippet always waited across the street beneath the awning in the shade. She had plans to visit him again that afternoon and couldn't wait to hear his voice.

"Move on." The order was given, and Poole moved out, Swan shimmied to the left and Noble took two steps forward to the top of the stairs.

Poole was the first to respond, he heard a whizzing sound, turned, and fell to the ground. Swan, startled by the move, responded by whipping out his Colt. 45 and diving to the ground. Poole saw the impact of the bullet as it thudded into Noble's chest. The impact made a sickening sound. Noble fell backward on the sheriff who was knocked to the ground. Blood squirted out of Noble's chest like water from a fountain. He made a sickening guttural sound. It was the painful and surprised sound of death. It was as vicious as the death he meted out to Jenkins.

Wells scrambled from beneath Noble. "Where did that come from?"

Poole jumped to his feet and ran across the road. Millie Tippet ran toward the scene of carnage. Screaming and crying like a mother who had lost a child. Swan rolled over in the dirt and sprang to his feet. "Are you alright, Sheriff?"

"Fine," he pointed to Poole. "Follow him," he said as he struggled to stand.

Swan nodded and moved off. He soon caught up to Poole. "Where did the shot come from?"

"This way I think," but the truth was he didn't know.

Millie reached Noble. He was dead. Blood continued to pump out of the gaping wound. His heart has been punctured. It was a perfect shot. Blood ran out of his chest. She tried to stop the blood by pressing her tear-stained handkerchief over the wound, but it was no good. His face was pale and clammy. She placed her hands on his face and called his name. "Timothy. Timothy." Oblivious of the movement of the lawmen around her.

She looked up as a crowd of onlookers began to encroach. She yelled at them. "Get away from here you vultures."

They ignored her of course and watched her while she sobbed.

Von Klaus was quickly on the scene.

James Fallon wrapped his arms around Millie, and she fell into him, and he guided her away from her admirer's body.

Noble was quickly pronounced dead. Wells and Poole scoured the town in search of the shooter, while Swan quickly mounted and scouted the western horizon beyond the town limits. It seemed to him the most logical place for the shot to come from.

Purcell and Boggins took control of the scene and moved the crowd back. McBean took one look outside the window and returned to the chambers. The death reinforced everything he had come to believe was wrong with the world.

Noble's big eyes stared at the sky. His once moist lips were now dry.

Someone was heard to have said, "that's justice."

McBean drank until he passed out.

CHAPTER 64

The funeral of Wiley Johns was a somber affair. It was postponed to the following morning, and there were only a handful of mourners. The air was cold, and a low and dark cloud precipitated a misty rain. Smoke escaped chimneys and felt its way into the air as Johns was lowered into the ground. Reverend Blair was solemn and though his service was swift, the message was clear. Men and women coveted sin because they lacked a sense of belonging, due to the breakdown of community.

Johns deserved a greater send off, but quite often people who deserve to be eulogized depart this world with little recognition. Often, it's the people who deserve to be eulogized which are often forgotten. But no one truly deserves anything. Life unfolds upon the world and chance meets the edge of humanity. Choices are made, and actions are taken. Morality underpins everything people do, and or don't do. Somewhere amongst the calamity people manage to interact peacefully. The contradictions between the needs of society do not always align with the wants of the people that are governed by the law. There are rule breakers, as there are law abiding citizens. The dividing line is a shared understanding of the virtue of living in a world that cherishes distinct cultural values. The edge of time had turned, and the citizens of Rocksprings felt the tightening of the screw.

The folks of Rocksprings were fearful. Once again, another man was murdered, in broad daylight this time. Not that there would be many people that mourned his passing, except Millie Tippet of course, but it was the cold and deliberate act that troubled folks. They locked themselves indoors. Only a few braved the elements and the troubles of the outside world. The cold-blooded murder of Noble was the culmination of events precipitated by the deaths of Deadeye Dave, Miles Hammond, Wiley Johns, Thomas Bland, and the death of the man that started it all, Jake Jenkins.

The three lawmen scoured the town for hours after the shooting of Noble. Wells kept vigil within the town limits while Swan and Poole searched the surrounding area for signs. They spoke to everybody they saw and went to nearby ranches to question the inhabitants, but their inquiries drew a blank slate. Still, the men searched well into the night. They were exhausted when they called a halt to the search, an hour before dawn.

When they rose after only a few hours rest they continued their quest to find the killer. It was a job made that much more difficult by contrasting speculations as to the origin of the shooter. The rain added an extra layer of complexity, as this hampered the chance of finding tracks. When Wells closed the squeaky rusty gate of Boot Hill behind, he sighed wearily. He had no idea what to do next. There was still another funeral to be had, and that was of Noble. It would have to wait, as there were more pressing matters.

Cletus Cloverfield sat at his large desk. The drunken and pathetic figure of a man, Owen Restful, was lying on the floor of the spare room, drunk as a tally whacker. His snoring could be heard from the opposite end of the house. Across the desk from the lawyer was Millie Tippet. He had sent a request for her to meet with him regarding the last will and testament of Timothy Noble.

"Miss Tippet, thanks for meeting on such short notice. I understand that there is never really an ideal time to discuss such matters, however, I have made travel plans and intend to conclude business before I leave."

She nodded. "I understand, Mr. Cloverfield."

"Miss Tippet, Mr. Noble had a sizable sum of money in an account in Lubbock. This was from the sale of his parents' house, as you well know. I witnessed Noble's last will and testament, and he leaves you his meager belongings which can be gathered from the jail, and the money left in his account, minus my fee of course."

He handed her the letter which she stared at for a while, opened it with a letter opener placed conveniently on the desk in front of her. She paused before reading the letter, and cried when she finished, folded, and grasped it tightly with both hands and wept some more. After a silent moment she spoke. "He wasn't in his right state of mind, was he, when he killed that man?"

CC shook his head. "No Miss. Tippet, he was not. The law has got it wrong."

"You were never going to win that case, were you? I mean no one was ever going to win."

The statement made him feel better. "No ma'am. A man had died violently, and the people wanted justice, well their definition of it anyway. That meant hanging. His fate was sealed from the beginning."

She stood and wiped her eyes with a clean and blood free handkerchief. "I will make necessary arrangements for the transfer of your fee."

"Thanks, ma'am. Will you be staying in Rocksprings?"

She smiled weakly. "I always considered myself duty bound to stay to tend to my parents' graves like a good Christian should do, but the last six weeks has taught me a lot about who I am, what I expect from others, and most importantly what I expect from myself. I am leaving, sir, but not before I say my farewells. I expect that I will return someday, but I can't say with any confidence when that will be. What about you, sir?"

He leaned back in his chair and folded his arms across his chest. "When my affairs have been tended to, I plan to head east. I can't say how far I will get, but the further I get away from this backwater the better I will feel."

He stood to bid her goodbye. He held out his hand and she took it in her dainty gloved palm. "Farewell, Miss.

Tippett, may the sunshine on the other side of today." He bowed slightly.

She smiled, and without saying a word she left him standing alone in his office regretting every decision he had ever made. Overcome with a sense of anger he marched down the hallway and opened the door to the doctor's room. He grabbed the drunk man's belongings and stuffed them into the valise he brought with him. He walked, most determinedly to the front door and tossed his valise as far as he could. Returning to the room he grabbed his expert witness from the seat of the pants and the scruff of the neck, hustled him to the door and threw him into the street.

CHAPTER 65

Time moved quickly or was that people? Festus Rasmussen was bored. As far as he was concerned, he had waited long enough, and it was time to move on. He knew he wouldn't, he was simply restless, that is all. He spent the day lounging in the shade and swimming in the cool water. Boredom had caused him to eat more than he should have, but what else was there for him to do, aside from sleep? He couldn't read, so that leisurely activity was off limits. He threw rocks at makeshift targets and even took a pot shot at a few prairie chickens. He managed to wing one, and it flopped hopelessly to the side and limped around and around in circles until he swatted it with a stick a few times. He spent the afternoon whistling and plucking the old bird.

His bay whinnied and he stood dropping the plucked bird into the dust. He looked around, until he saw the source of the bay's interest. A mile, a mile, and a half away, heading from the south-west, a lone figure, rode easily in his direction. He smiled, cleansed the bird in the water, and hung it from the tree. It was a careless move for the flies were soon attracted to the smell. Rasmussen reloaded his pistol, holstered it, and waited.

The rider was tall, and lanky. He had shoulder length hair and sported some stubble. His eyes were as keen as obsidian. The top three buttons of his shirt were undone to let the cool breeze, what there was of it, cool him down. His Stetson was battered and bruised.

Rasmussen leaned against the tree and smiled in return. "Just in time," he said, "I was about to start cooking dinner. The rider halted twenty yards away, and let his bones settle before trying to dismount. Festus moved across and took the reins. He was waiting anxiously, yet he dared not ask. Not yet.

"I'm hungry," the man said. "I'll take care of my horse, you just get that bird cooking, before the flies eat it."

Rasmussen, who already had a low fire going, added tinder to the flames and it quickly engulfed the dry wood.

"Put some coffee on while you're at it."

The big man obeyed, while the other removed the saddle, and hitched the horse. He stripped down to his long johns and jumped into the cool water letting out a satisfied wince from the start of the cool water. Thirty minutes later in which the men didn't speak, the stranger redressed and sat down to a hot cup of coffee and burned bird.

"It's as tough as old boot leather," Rasmussen muttered.

The man ate ravenously and chewed like a mangy cur on a rotten piece of meat. When he ate his fill, and finished his first cup of coffee, he looked at Rasmussen, patted him on the shoulder and smiled.

"Are you going to tell me what happened?"

The man continued to eat. Festus became quite animated. "Deadeye, tell me, did you, do it? Is he?" He left the sentence unfinished.

Deadeye smiled as wide as a pleased man is entitled to. "D.E.D, DED."

Deadeye proceeded to tell his partner how the killing went down. He waited patiently, like a lioness stalking its prey until the right opportunity. The shooting spot was six hundred yards west of the courthouse. It was late afternoon. The sun was behind him. No one was expecting anything to happen, after all he was dead.

From within a small copse of sparse trees he waited. He aimed his Whitworth rifle, the same rifle he used in the Civil War, in which he made a name for himself as a sharpshooter. He smiled and pulled the trigger. Deadeye elaborated of course and made the story appeal to his partner's craving for such stories. When the laughing died down Rasmussen was out of things to say, but there was something else he needed to get off his chest. It had been bothering him ever since Reverend Blair's words touched his conscience, and that was murder.

"What about Buddy Franks?"

"Only you and I know about that, Festus. That'll be the last time his name is mentioned."

He nodded. Deadeye was right. He was always right.

"Did you do everything I told you to?"

His partner explained about the meeting with the banker, the sale of the mines and the transfer of funds.

"How was my funeral?"

"Just swell. I cried like a baby. There's a cross with your name on it. I carved it myself."

"Do they suspect anything?"

"Not a thing. It was a perfect plan, Deadeye, simply perfect."

They laughed together for a while and sat in silence.

The night fell quickly, and they were consumed in darkness. The flames of the fire licked the sky. Deadeye licked his lips, sipped some brandy, and settled into his blanket. The moon was high in the sky and the evening was peaceful. He quickly fell asleep. Festus, on the other hand, spent most of the day napping and was wide awake. His thoughts weren't on Deadeye, though he was mighty glad to see him. The man made him feel safe. Nor were his thoughts on Noble, after all he was glad, he was dead. The image of Deadeye shooting Buddy Franks haunted him. He could smell the smoke of the shotgun. He could also smell the burned flesh of Franks. He had played his part well. He had done everything he was told to do.

Staring at the stars across the wide expanse of the sky. The gentle snoring of his friend beside him. He began to consider, for the first time in his life, the possibility of something beyond the here and now, and if the reverend was right then he needed to find a way to repent.

THE END

DED